PICK A COLOUR

By the same author

FICTION
How to Pronounce Knife (2020)

POETRY
Cluster (2019)
Light (2013)
Found (2007)
Small Arguments (2003)

PICK A

Souvankham Thammavongsa

COLOUR

BLOOMSBURY PUBLISHING
LONDON · OXFORD · NEW YORK · NEW DELHI · SYDNEY

BLOOMSBURY PUBLISHING
Bloomsbury Publishing Plc
50 Bedford Square, London, WC1B 3DP, UK
Bloomsbury Publishing Ireland Limited,
29 Earlsfort Terrace, Dublin 2, D02 AY28, Ireland

BLOOMSBURY, BLOOMSBURY PUBLISHING and the Diana logo
are trademarks of Bloomsbury Publishing Plc

First published in 2025 by Knopf Canada, an imprint of
Penguin Random House Canada
First published in Great Britain 2025

Copyright © Souvankham Thammavongsa, 2025

Souvankham Thammavongsa is identified as the author of this work in accordance
with the Copyright, Designs and Patents Act 1988.

This is a work of fiction. Names and characters are the product of the author's
imagination and any resemblance to actual persons, living or dead,
is entirely coincidental

Acknowledgment is made to the Editors of *The Walrus* in whose pages some of the
writing was first printed.

All rights reserved. No part of this publication may be: i) reproduced or transmitted
in any form, electronic or mechanical, including photocopying, recording or by
means of any information storage or retrieval system without prior permission in
writing from the publishers; or ii) used or reproduced in any way for the training,
development or operation of artificial intelligence (AI) technologies, including
generative AI technologies. The rights holders expressly reserve this publication
from the text and data mining exception as per Article 4(3) of the Digital Single
Market Directive (EU) 2019/790

A catalogue record for this book is available from the British Library

ISBN: HB: 978-1-5266-1048-5; eBook: 978-1-5266-1050-8

2 4 6 8 10 9 7 5 3 1

Typeset by: Erin Cooper
Printed and bound in Great Britain by Clays Ltd, Elcograf S.p.A

MIX
Paper | Supporting
responsible forestry
FSC® C018072

To find out more about our authors and books visit www.bloomsbury.com
and sign up for our newsletters
For product safety related questions contact productsafety@bloomsbury.com

Everyone is ugly. I should know. I look at people all day.

They come to me with their faces. Shoving themselves forward. Demanding something be done. Wanting me to do something about it. Anything, anything really. "Please," they say.

Now, I don't do magic. I can't make things appear or disappear. I can only work with what's in front of me.

And there's a lot there. In front of me.

Most want to get rid of hair above the lip or on the chin. They want me to work in the narrow space of a brow. Control the centre line. Hair—that is, if they have any—is an easy thing to remove from a face. You just pull. Of course, how you pull, and what you pull it with, matters. So does the angle. Use wax or thread or tweezers. Watch the direction hair grows, and pull.

Faces give so much away. Feelings, especially. The muscles most used will carve a line. One's habits are there for everyone to see. The purse of a lip, a wrinkle holding space for a sneer or smile, a frown cast so often across a face it remains.

Most people don't know what's good for them, and when they think they do they're mostly wrong. I listen and tell them about the goods we have. The cleansers, toners, serums, essences, gels and creams and oils and masks and moisturizers. I come up with a way to deal with the sun and the damage.

Now, I have to be careful with that word, *damage*, and how I use it. A helpful suggestion can turn suddenly into a bad feeling. And people don't forgive you for giving them bad feelings. Especially about themselves.

Then when I'm done with their faces, and they're not cheap, they give me their hands and toes. Who knows where those things have been, but I can't think too much about that. I clean and shape and buff and polish.

Looking at the two of us, them sitting on a chair above me, and me down low, you'd think I am not in charge. But I am. I know everything about them, whether or not they tell me. You look at something long enough and you begin to see everything in its details. And you'd be surprised what people tell you when they think you are a stranger and they are never going to see you again.

1

I live in a world of Susans. I got name tags for everyone who works at this nail salon, and on every one is printed the name "Susan." So many girls come and go. I don't want to bother getting new name tags each time. Besides, you know, it's never difficult to pronounce a name like Susan.

None of our clients notice. They come in and we are ready and set to work. That's all that matters to them. We all have black shoulder-length hair and wear black T-shirts and black pants. We are, more or less, the same height, too.

And, anyway, the clients will never be wrong when they ask for Susan. Dear Susan is always available and at your service! Susan never takes a day off and Susan is never fully booked if it's you who called for her. Susan, our dear, sweet Susan, always makes time for you.

The Susans and I are friendly, the way you are with someone you work with, with someone you have to see every day. I like to keep my distance, not get too close to any of them. They aren't family. Even with family, I like to keep my distance.

I did my time.

The brightly lit box we work in is called "Susan's." There are others like us scattered around the city, and some are just a few doors down from us. But we're the best. It's no lie and I'm not kidding anybody when I say that. We're the best. I get people in and out, in and out, and so do the Susans.

I'm in charge, and I do what I want. I can do it all. I am the first to arrive and the last one to leave, and I never take a day off. I have got four girls—Mai, Nok, Annie, and a new girl coming, Noi. I know our names sound the same, but because I know what their names mean in our language they aren't the same to me. Any one of us can answer the phone and take appointments. Only the ones with more experience can do the manicures and pedicures, facials or waxings. And someone's always on standby, just a call away.

You can't fit much in the shop. Five chairs lined up along the pink wall, four stations, and our centrepiece—a white leather chair that leans back and spins. The chair is mostly for facials, waxings, threading, but we can do mani-pedis there too. We usually reserve it for someone who wants the works. Or just to make someone feel special. But they can sit anywhere in the shop, and we can go to them and do it all from there. There can't be more than three of us, each with a client. Face, hands, feet. Any more than that and I lose track of who is doing what and when.

And I don't like to lose track, to not know.

My day begins at seven in the morning. When I open my eyes I know exactly what I will see. The ceiling. There's a crack in there. It has the shape of a single black hair with a split end.

I live in this tiny apartment on the top floor, right above the shop. Hardwood floors, a kitchen and bathroom with a shower and tub. It is just one room, but I don't need that much space. There used to be some plants, but I didn't care for them. So I don't have anything like that around.

I am alone because I want to be. If you want to know—because people like to know stuff like this where I work—I'm not married. And I don't have kids. I am a family of one. You can be that, you know. A family of one. I could have had what everyone else has, but it didn't turn out. I am about to turn forty-two. It's a good age to be. I don't have to become anything anymore.

It is the middle of August.

I should open a window, but I don't want the hot air from outside to get in. It already feels like I'm inside a mouth. All wet, so little room, and there's no place to go but down. I do love it at the shop. I can't remember the last time I spent any time away from it. I live down there, really, spend more hours there than I do here. Been here, on my own, for just about five years. It's a solid number, isn't it. I got my start working for someone else, watching how they ran the whole thing. And before that, I had a whole other life. I was a boxer. My dad got me into it. Convinced I could go to the Olympics or do something like that. I never made it that far, didn't win anything.

And I hurt a girl real bad one time. Put her in a coma for a few weeks. My coach, Murch, said I was glorious, but that's not glory to me. Once you've been in the ring, you don't forget it. It doesn't take much for a memory to strike me. A sweat bead on someone's forehead, the length of someone's arm, a bruise. I'm quick to read people, see if I can take them out. And that thing I have been told—protect yourself at all times—I still do it. Just can't let anybody in. I'm not too hard up on any feelings about leaving the whole thing. Why turn my face toward something that spit me out? Anyway, I aged out of it real quick, too. I didn't know what to do with myself after and kicked around, doing various jobs, living in a bunch of small towns. But I missed the city. The streetcar, the pigeons, the sound of the ambulance.

Maybe my old coach felt sorry for me. Saw how I was spit out into nothing and wanted to help. Told me about one of the guys at the gym. Said the guy had a sister who owned a nail salon and if I needed work she'd give me something to do. I was twenty-five then. For a long time, I answered phones and did just the basics. I shared a room with a bunch of girls who worked at the nail salon. Then one night, Rachel—the guy's sister—said, "You're the oldest girl here. I don't know what you're thinking, but I don't want to grow old with you." I never thought of myself as old. I felt the same as I was when I first started. But I wasn't outside looking at my own face like she was. The way she was looking at me. I just felt like I wasn't welcome anymore. She cut my shifts after that. Part-time. And then suddenly there wasn't work for me. Twelve years, I was with her, and I was spit out of that too.

I still had my finger then.

It was winter when I got this place and moved in upstairs. The trees across the street, in the park, looked like upside-down trees. The roots frayed with nowhere to go. I know the feeling and when I saw that I knew this place had to be mine.

I hear the phone ring downstairs. It means someone out there wants me today.

2

I turn on the light switch by the entrance. *Flick*. And it all comes to life. Everything is as I left it. The five chairs, the four stations, the centrepiece.

I walk over to the phone.

See its blinking red light. A message. Before I check that, I move over to face the computer screen and look at the appointments. Who here on the list is new to me, who might be familiar. I think of what we booked them for, and I think of what else they might ask for when they're here and if we might have time to squeeze that in. This computer is old and it could give out any time. I keep a logbook right next to it. The book is a black, leather-bound, sturdy thing that holds everything the computer does, but it runs on nothing. I reach out and pat the cover like it is someone's back.

I look at the screen again to see which girl is on the floor with me.

Is she experienced or might I have to step in and help out, leaving my own client? Will the client I am with be patient and understanding when I am out of service to them for a bit? Will the girl be slow, will the girl and client match, and what to do if there's a blow-up between the two of them? Can she talk?

When I was just starting out, Rachel asked me, "What's your take on babies?"

"Don't want them."

"And affairs."

"Don't have them."

"Married people."

"Wouldn't want to be them."

She laughed at my answers, and said, "Well, in our line of work, you better get used to hearing about babies, affairs, love, married people, weddings. And you better look interested when it comes up."

"Why?"

"They come for the talk. Talk they can't get anywhere else. They don't come back for the nails."

"How can you stand it?"

"You think that shit is dumb? Beneath you? Is that it? You motherfucker." Rachel said that affectionately. "This shit is our fucking glory."

"Don't you hate that anyone can just walk in here? Expect us to be things?"

"It's no different than any other job. You decide what you want to be to them."

I do what I usually do this time of day. Give Mai a call. Go over who we've got coming in today. She likes to know that stuff before she gets in so she's ready to go. She doesn't even say hello or anything like that. She picks up and just says, "What've we got? Who've you got coming in today."

I tell her the pitcher's booked his usual hour.

"Anyone else? Anyone else."

I tell her it's just him. The one guy for the first hour.

"We shouldn't just do his hands. We always do that. Let's get his feet done. Pluck his brows. Shave his face. Book him in for next time."

I nod, and realize she can't see me.

"You listening to me? You got this?"

"Yeah. I got it."

I've known Mai for what feels like forever. It was always like this. Us, talking. She barks something at me and I take it in. She reminds me a little of Murch. When I first got to his boxing gym, I was little, or itty-bitty, is what he called it. He had his favourites—his boys, his champs.

Thing was, none of them were any good. Were told all their lives they were good. By their mothers, their sisters, their cousins, their girls. Always someone telling them, in their corner. And the minute they didn't hear that, always another woman telling them.

I didn't have that.

Murch said to get in there, in the ring, and try anyway, that's a champ. "I know one when I see one," he said then.

But he's got a new itty-bitty now. I see him posting stories of her on Instagram. Her face pops up for five seconds. I don't know why I even bother to look. Haven't talked to him in years. It is kind of hard to watch it all unfold in real time. This bright, shiny new thing. Anything she does, like put on a glove, there's a story about it. When I was his boxer not a lot of people knew about it. Everything I did, I did in the ring.

"Who else?" Mai asks. "That pitcher bringing in his friend?"

"Won't know until they get here, but we don't have him booked."

"We see him, we book him."

I stare at the computer screen, and quickly run my eyes down the list of clients who have booked appointments. The baseball guy, the waitress, a bridal shower—will need the extra girl for that one—Marla, Janet, ugh, and a new one, Vanessa.

"You think we'll get any walk-ins?" I can hear her smile even though I can't see her face.

"We always get some walk-ins."

"Let's get them in and out. In and out. Twenty minutes max."

I don't say anything.

"You listening to me?"

"Right here."

"And the new girl. The one coming in today. Just tell her what to do. Tell her what to do and she's going to do it. And if she doesn't then we'll just get a new one next week. Give her a few days to see. Just see." I hear a silence on the line and take that as her having left our talk. She gets off the phone like she gets on it.

I imagine the new girl in this space, moving around. Her quiet, rapid little steps and thin shoulders. Her pointed chin. She's young.

When I was interviewing a bunch of them, there were other girls with more experience. This girl had none. She admitted to it, though. She admitted that. Right up front. Said she was nineteen. Just had a baby. The father, married to someone else to begin with, isn't involved. Said she just wanted to work. Said she had no one. She said that. In a job interview. Anyone who can tell you about their life in the first five minutes of meeting them is someone who can work here. You can't teach that. You either have it or you don't.

I think of unlocking the door, but stop.

Don't want anyone to just come in at this hour. Too early. Anyone coming in at this time is trouble. Better not leave the door unlocked. I'll unlock it when I can actually see that the new girl is standing outside.

I will have the new girl at the desk. Answering phones, taking messages, booking appointments, getting water bottles. She can't work and get into it like we do because she doesn't know the job yet.

There's traffic outside. Heavy. Cars—little ones that look like candy and seat just two—vans, trucks, big-wheeled pickups, bikers, taxis, all pressed front to back to front. They form a straight line on both sides of the street. Honks. There's an ambulance, but it's in the distance. I can tell because none of the cars have moved to the side, made way for anything coming to pass. I glance at the traffic light and it's red. Traffic-light red. That could be a nail colour, couldn't it. All the cars have one driver and no one else in them.

I notice the empty.

I see a head turn my way. I nod at the person in the car, but they don't nod back. They turn their face away and look straight ahead again, like nothing happened. When you look at someone, that's something. You nod, you wave. Do something to show you saw them. Can't knock them for being like that. I'm that way too sometimes.

It would be nice to be thought of, though.

Maybe later tonight we will come across their mind like static does on a television screen. A brief interruption in their daily programming. A place they might check out on the way home from work or while they're out and about on a weekend. A gift certificate, perhaps. Something to tell friends about.

There is a pigeon at the edge of the curb, and it's by itself. It gives me a strange feeling when I only see one pigeon. Where are the others? Are they nearby? Its head bobs and weaves like it is shadowboxing.

I used to feed the pigeons when I first got this place. I don't want anything around me to go hungry. Then I noticed all the clumps of white droppings around the entrance. Takes forever to clean that stuff from the sidewalk. And I don't mean to give myself any extra work scrubbing the sidewalk of that.

I'll get the new girl to scare the pigeons away. Tell her any time she sees one to get out there and shove it away. They can't be crowding around our door. It's a bad look.

I remember the blinking red light. And check our messages. There's one. I listen. Heavy breathing. That's all.

I delete the message.

We get these all the time. And I think nothing of it. A wrong number, a butt-dial.

I feel a presence by the door and look up, and there she is. The new girl.

3
—

I let her in.

The new girl didn't knock, or do anything to call attention to herself. Probably thinks knocking on glass is being too loud. Probably thinks when she breathes she's making too much noise. She's just standing there now, smiling at me, waving her right hand. The way she waves her hand tells me everything about her. Quick, eager to please.

She's dressed as I told her to dress. Black pants, black shirt, black running shoes. Her hair is black and shoulder-length.

I motion for her to follow me. We take a few steps past the front desk and walk down a short hallway, to the back. I point, tell her to put her phone and bag in the back room. "No one goes in there but us," I say. She goes in there alone.

When she comes back, I start right away. I don't like to chit-chat, no how-are-yous, no coddling. No tell-me-about-yourself-now. Just get to it.

I wave the new girl over to our wall of nail polish, close to our one big window. I ask her, testing, "Are they all full?" Pointing to the four rows. They are at just the right height. Not too high or too low, otherwise no one will pick those colours. We have so many colours. Eighty-three to be exact. Oranges, reds, pinks, purples, and everything in between. It all makes me think of food, and I want to grab them all and stuff them into my mouth.

She squints. Takes her time to answer. I spot a few, but I don't say anything. "This one," she says, bringing her hand up to the bottle. "This one's not full."

I then notice that her fingernails are painted red. I point at them, and say, "What is *that*?" She looks at what I'm looking at, and doesn't know what I am talking about.

I yell, "Your nails!"

"Oh. Sorry?"

She apologizes, but she doesn't know what for.

"They're *red*!" I say, my eyes bulging. She has to have bare nails!

"What do you mean?" She folds all her fingers at the knuckle to get a look at the colour, and asks, "What's wrong with just red?"

"There's no such thing as *just* red."

She stares at me blankly, like we are not speaking the same language.

"There's apple red," I insist, "cherry red, pen red, sexy

red, demure red, pale red, lipstick red, shy red, hot red, blood red, car-brake red, swimsuit red, New Year's red, strawberry red, wet-paint red, gummy red, rose red, flower red—now rose is a flower but it's not flower red, it's its own red, rose red. Then there are other shades of red like orange red, purple red, blue red, yellow red..."

"Okay," Noi finally says. "I got it."

"Do you? Do you got it? You better know these reds because if you don't you're not going to make it here. You better know your reds when you're out here on the floor and it's go time."

She doesn't say anything.

It is a waste for us to wear nail polish ourselves. We wash our hands so often it gets chipped away. And red is the worst colour for us to wear. What happens when we use nail polish removal? We use it on every client. If our own polish rubs off it stains the client's hands and goes into the grooves of the palm print and it's so hard to remove once it goes in there. The skin there is rough.

And worse, what if they want to see a nail polish colour and ask us to paint ours to show them?

We can't simply paint on top of our own nail polish. It wouldn't be exact. And what's going to happen when they choose that colour thinking it's the same shade and then it isn't because it's been layered on top of a red? We'd have to remove it on all ten fingernails. Waste.

I bring over nail polish remover and she knows what to do. I have to keep it moving, so we get back to it, and I tell her first thing we do each morning is make sure each nail polish bottle is full. And if it isn't, we fill it with nail polish thinner.

There's nothing more embarrassing for us than using nail polish from a bottle that is almost empty. Shaking and turning the bottle upside down, tapping its bottom for it to burp out a colour. Worse is when the dry air gets sealed in there and dries out the nail polish into one hard clump so it cannot be used at all.

Once a client is set on a colour, it's difficult to change their mind. And, besides, we don't like to disappoint them—if their heart is set on a colour, it's going to be that colour.

Noi doesn't need to know this yet. She has big wide eyes. When you talk to her, they get wider, as if she takes the whole world in through the space her eyes provide. I try not to tell her too much. Hasn't got the kind of head to hold it all in. For now, she just needs to know the bottles have to look full.

"You see this?"

She nods.

"The bottle's face has to look forward. All lined up against the wall, it looks neat and new this way."

After we are done painting, we bring the polishes back. Don't leave them lying around. It looks a mess. And we don't want mess here. Neat and clean. My index finger shoots up and glides along the air to demonstrate a straight line.

Every client who walks in is told to pick a colour. Remember to tell them that. Get them to come to this wall and pick. One for their hands, one for their feet. Sometimes they pick the same colour, and that's fine.

"Pick a colour," she says in a quiet whisper to no one.

I bring her over to our stations.

Cotton balls here, filing pads here, moisturizers, oils. Turn all the bottles at the station so that the pump is facing us, and make sure the opening is not clogged.

When it gets clogged, you have to pump two or three times to unclog it. The moisturizer can get stuck in the nozzle. Pump it a few times and a big *plop* lands in your palm. We want to avoid that sound in front of a client. If there's anything disgusting here, it's that sound. Don't want to hear it.

I repeat, "Pump. Here."

I tell her I'm left-handed so at my station everything's on the right.

She doesn't notice my finger.

—

We move over to the centrepiece, our spinning chair, by the wall. I say, "We do facials here."

She nods.

"This jar with the blue liquid?"

"Uh-huh."

"Our tools. Soak them overnight. Take them out and wipe them clean. Have them ready for us at the stations."

I point to the pot of wax.

"Wax. On," I say. I turn it on so she sees where the switch is. Now it will be ready to go by the time we have our first appointment, whether or not it's something we have them down for. Be ready. They might ask if we can add that.

We walk back to the front desk, facing the door. I open the cash register there and say, "They'll use the machine to pay, but if they use cash put it in here."

I tell her there should be one hundred dollars in the till. Any more and end of the day we deposit that at the bank. If we get robbed they'll only have one hundred dollars.

"Robbed?" she asks, innocently. "That happens here?" I can see she hasn't thought of this, working in a store that has cash.

I tell her, coldly, "A few times." And add, without any worry, "Just give them everything. We can make one hundred back easy."

I press the button on the credit card machine.

After a moment, I tell her, "Takes a while before it starts." We want to have this machine ready to go for the client to pay, otherwise they tell you they'll come back later because they're in a hurry, and then they don't.

"What happens," she worries, looking around, "when we run out of paper?" I like that this matters to her. It should. Receipts are our birth certificates. It's proof. Proof that we were there that day and with whom and at what hour. Proof that someone paid and that tip was ours. Without a receipt, who knows what really happened? Someone could say we were never there at all. To do work, and to not have a receipt? Might as well not exist.

Here.

I open the top desk drawer and take out a new roll. Underneath it are some children's drawings. They are pretty close to the real thing, if you ask me. Children notice one thing and exaggerate it on the page. Arms and legs are never the same length and height. Everyone is always standing, never sitting down. Always facing the page with their whole face. They are never turned to the side. Hair is a squiggle of circles or curls or blunt bangs. Or none at all. I notice they never used the gold-coloured crayon. I guess nothing ever calls for being gold.

Those kids liked drawing us.

One Susan they drew had a large chest—that must be Mai. Another had a nostril bigger than the other one. Maybe that's their mother. And when it came to me, it was easy. I was the one with the nine fingers. I was a single line in the middle. My arms and legs were splayed out. I had a letter O for my mouth. Dots for each eye. And one nostril not much bigger than the eyes.

They got all our hair right. Black.

Nok's kids gave me these drawings at the end of one of her shifts. I put them in here. Seemed cruel to throw their drawings out. I even kept their colouring. When they didn't want to draw, they wanted to colour. We had nothing to colour so I drew something. Just a giant circle. And inside the giant circle were other little circles.

I gave them rules for our colouring game. You can use the same colour, but it must appear somewhere else, and at least one circle apart. No circle is to be surrounded by a circle of the same colour. That kept them busy.

"So cute!" Noi says, peering into the drawer. "Who made these?"

Nok hasn't been showing up for her shifts. A reason we had to start looking for a new girl. But I don't tell her that. I just say, "A couple of kids."

I move on.

I put the roll of paper next to the register so whoever works it doesn't ask anyone where the paper is.

I check the pens. There's enough ink in each one.

As I show the new girl around, I put together a list of things we might run out of soon. It's for me when I do a supply run—it's good to have a list ready. Just like the clients being in and out, I want myself moving that way too.

The new girl wants to ask me something, but I see her hesitate. I don't like to guess at what people want to say. If they have something to say, they should say it. I think she can sense me thinking this and she says quietly, "Are you worried about the one-star rating you have?"

I pretend to laugh, and it sounds like I am trying to blow out something I've got stuck in my nose, and when I come out of it, I say, "—Oh, don't you worry about that. Every one of them? Fucking hypocrites. We get them back. We get them all back. We never lose one. You just tell them 'ten dollars.' Better price somewhere, have a complaint, we are taking too long, not happy, new place opening up—just tell them 'ten dollars.'"

"Ten dollars," she repeats.

"We never lose them. They all come back."

I watch everything closely. The girls don't like it. Even when they know what they are doing, it can make them feel like they don't. Makes a person nervous to be looked at. Simple things like picking up a tool makes them pause and wonder if it's the right one. Just my looking says to them maybe they don't know what they know. So I watch closely, but I don't let them see me.

I look at the clock on the wall. Its two golden hands spread apart like legs.

"Showtime," I say.

I give the new girl her name tag. *Susan*, it says.

4

Just the basics. That's what we offer. We use only what people have. Don't draw or make or add any fancy designs. All that stuff adds to our cost and takes up too much time. We don't want them here all day. Like I said, we want them in and out.

I started with just a couple of girls on the floor with me. Someone to answer the phone when I can't. Someone to take a walk-in. Keep the price low, so they are likely to pay us up with cash. The girls keep what they make an hour and they keep their tips. I don't take any of it. And I don't rent out the chairs to them and come collecting after their rent is paid up like those other places. I take care of them. I'm no cheat.

This early in the day, the sidewalks fill with kids on their way to camp. They all have big backpacks. They all look like they're moving house and they're taking everything with them on their backs.

One kid stops right outside our window and waves to

me. I wave back. Then the kid pounces forward and presses two sweaty palms on the glass and runs away laughing.

The oil prints the grooves and lines on the glass, smudging the shine that should be there. I look over at the new girl, but she's tapping at her phone. She doesn't notice that I am looking at her. Can't feel it, the way Mai can feel my look. I grab a spray bottle, and go outside to get rid of the stain. If I don't, I know I will look at that spot all day.

As I am making my way back, I see her. It's Mai. Her name is short and sounds easy to say, but if you pronounce it wrong, it will mean burned or brand-new or penalty. Her name means wood in our language. "Because it's everywhere. That's why," she likes to say, triumphantly, when she's asked why she was named that.

I study Mai. I like the way she carries herself. Confident, assured. She isn't afraid of anyone. And if there's a blow-up between us on the floor, she soon forgets that it ever happened. Doesn't hold a grudge. Knows it's the work, not me.

She lives across town. A forty-minute bus ride. But she doesn't complain about the ride and is never late. Reliable. Her mother lives with her, and they're close. I don't know how that works. I don't think I could live with my mother, if you want to know. I can't even spend a few hours with her. Her breathing gets too loud for me. It's all I hear. And her smacking lips. She's either talking or eating.

When Mai gets closer, she says, "Hey." She peers through the glass window and sees the new girl sitting there. She says, "The new one."

"First shift. Noi is her name."

"Noi. Poor thing. Looks like it too," she says, measuring the girl with her eyes. Noi means tiny in our language. "Better be nice to her," she warns, as if to herself, her eyes looking at no one. She turns back to me, and adds, "You hear from Nok at all, she call?" She has been thinking of her too. We've all had to adjust our schedules to make up for Nok being a no-show.

I shake my head no.

She takes in my response and stares at me for a bit. She searches my face for a thought, but I don't add anything, and she heads inside. She nods over at the new girl and heads to the back. I follow Mai, and want to touch her hair. It needs a cut. It's grown longer than the rest of ours at the shop. And I don't like that.

"You need to cut your hair," I insist. "It's two inches longer than ours."

She turns around, glares at me, sucks her teeth.

"So? I can't help that. Just have to catch up with me that's all."

"It has to be cut," I say again, and Mai rolls her eyes at me. Her eyes are dark brown, almost black, like mine. They are expressive and do all her talking for her. It is almost like you can see her voice there before you hear it. I know what she thinks before she says it because it appears in how her eyes move.

And I know all their moves.

She gives the impression that she's beautiful, but it's not entirely true. When she talks to anyone, she leans toward them and makes her face available.

A face is never open and available to you like that unless you're going in for a kiss. If you are lonely, the way Mai's face moves in close, you feel it then—that no one's been that close for a long time now. Even if you're not interested in getting close, she presents it, and it gets people thinking about that.

I grab scissors and go to her.

Mai turns and gives me her back. I gently take her hair and cut two inches off. The scissors are sharp and so it doesn't take up much time.

Once it's done, she spins her front to me. She looks at me and peels off to the mirror in the bathroom. I follow her because I want to know what she thinks of what I did. I watch as she slowly turns her face a slight right and then a slight left, and says, "I make this look good."

Then she sticks out her chest, cups both her breasts and lifts them high and lets them go. They bounce like tennis balls.

She says, with a smile, "How's my tit game?" She looks over at my chest, and teases, "Not like your mosquitoes." I shrug, and correct her, "Pancakes. My pancakes." If anyone is going to comment on what they are, it should be me. My chest is sturdy and I like what I have. They serve me well.

Mai goes out to the front and this time greets the new girl sitting at the desk.

"First day, huh," she says, smiling.

The new girl smiles, too, but it's quick. If you blinked, you wouldn't notice it had been given to you.

"Don't let her scare you," Mai says, pointing her nose in my direction. "You got any problems, you just come to big sis right here," she says, pointing to the middle of her chest with her thumb. "I'll take care of you."

They look at each other for a while. Their eyes meet and the air between them seems to change into something warm and welcoming.

I don't want to take anything away from them, but if I am honest, I don't trust anyone who tells me to call them big sis. Or anyone who calls me big sis. You either are, or you aren't. A name doesn't change things.

And, anyway, watch big sis drop you when she wants anything for herself. Everyone's after their own.

I return them to the job, saying, "Who've we got? Coming in."

Mai walks over to our centrepiece. Her slow stride seems to call you to look at her. This annoys me somehow. This need of hers to be looked at all the time.

She knows this place, where everything is supposed to be. She quickly glances to her left at the nail bottles along the wall. All full. With her back to the street, she has a good view of the floor. She likes to look around, challenging, like a boxer feeling out the crowd, testing the ropes. See if they recognize any new feeling. Anything out of place.

Noi looks at the appointment log on the computer, and squints her eyes. Confused, she says, "Um. It says … Derek Jeter."

Mai, from the centrepiece, asks, "You know who that is?"

"Isn't he a baseball player?"

"Sure is. He comes here," Mai says, proudly. "To see us."

"Really? Is this true?"

"That's what it says, doesn't it?" Mai challenges.

"What does he come here for? Can't he hire someone who just travels around with him?"

"Cheap. Is what he is," I say, near the door, looking at the flow of traffic, at the pigeon, at the lock.

"And … and isn't he like retired?"

"Still got to get his nails done when he's in town."

Noi believes this.

"Quit playing with her," I tell Mai.

"Just messing," she says, grinning. "That's all."

It is tough being the new girl. You never know who is messing with you. You have to take what everyone tells you to be true.

I walk over to the desk and say to Noi, "Start making calls." I point to the computer screen. "Their phone numbers. Just go down the list. Leave messages."

Mai knows me and what I want. When I walk over to the centrepiece she's already brought me my tools, oils—everything I might need. Then she whispers to me, "You know he wants me." She thinks everyone wants her. Thing is, she's right most of the time. "Maybe he'll bring that little friend with him," she says, excitedly. "His friend wants me too."

I take my seat, look over my shoulder outside our window, and see that pigeon—the same one I saw earlier. It's still out there at the edge of the curb. Bobbing and weaving its head. I bet Mai would tell you it wants her, too.

5

The door opens.

Two men come in, one behind the other. I don't notice much about the second man. The one closest is wearing jeans and a plain blue T-shirt. He sees me and pulls his baseball cap low to cover his eyes. He bends three fingers and points the other two, and shoves them underneath his shirt so the lumps they form take the shape of a gun, and rushes over to the cash register, pointing at Noi. Her eyes spring toward me, pleading and helpless.

We all look on.

After a few seconds, we begin to laugh. Mai starts and is the loudest. My laugh is in there too, but I let Mai be the loudest. Noi realizes the joke.

It's the pitcher we have down as Jeter and his friend.

He takes out his hand from underneath his T-shirt and shows her the shape he made, both sides of it, waves it around, flattens out his hand, and then taps the desk, gives a winsome smile, tells her he was trying to give her a bit of adventure, and winks. The muscles on her face relax, returning her to herself. I have been wondering if I should describe her as beautiful. She might not be. She's just young.

I say to Noi, "He keeps the lights on in this place. Comes in after every practice, after every game." Jeter isn't his real name, of course. It's just to throw things off. A competing team or nosy reporter can't know what we do for the guy. It's a weakness that could be a game changer if it ever got out.

The pitcher doesn't speak our language so he asks me if I'm talking about him. Mai jumps in and tells him we are just saying how handsome he is.

He believes us, and smiles.

I continue to tell Noi, so she knows, we always have Jeter booked. "He needs to come in and get his nails filed down. It's the way he holds the ball to throw one of his pitches. The stitch on the ball gives him blisters."

A nail injury sounds like nothing, but it hurts in a way that you can't put out of your mind no matter what you are doing. People will pay anything to get the pain to go away. If it's damaged underneath, the pressure builds. We do what needs to be done to release it. If there's a crack, you glue where the split is. A crack splits a nail in two and as it grows it pulls the skin underneath it in two separate directions. For him, we never know what it's going to be until we see him. It has a life of its own so we keep an eye on it.

"Hey, hey," Mai says to me, "how long before he tells us how much he makes?"

"Five minutes," I say, confidently.

"Bets on."

He tells us how much he makes.

"Daaamn. He hasn't even sat down yet."

"Bet you he busts his balls that way too," I say, matter-of-factly. "Two pumps."

"Next time he makes his appointment, let's put him down as Two Pumps," Mai calls over to the desk. "Got that? Ahhha." She turns back to me. "Honestly, you think he makes what he says?"

The pitcher sits down at our centrepiece. He wasn't even invited and he goes there. It does look like a throne. That chair can make anyone sitting on it feel like royalty.

He takes off his ball cap and a levelled patch of brown hair sprouts all over his scalp. He points at me and says he called and left a message and did I get it?

I think of the blinking red light and the heavy breathing on the voicemail. Must have been him.

I look over at his friend, a shadow, really, standing near the register.

I have a soft spot for shadows. Anyone who wants to stay out of the spotlight has got my respect. Reminds me of some of the guys at the gym. I always thought boxing was about hitting something hard, but when I was there everyone was alone hitting lightly. Punching no one but the air in front of them. Bobbing and weaving. Everyone's opponent was invisible, a ghost. Figures without faces or bodies. Seen only to the person fighting. What was at stake was imagined and made up in the moment.

It felt urgent.

Their feet moved around. They circled and circled, making a small space appear on the floor, and they moved within that small space. They made, with their bodies, the outline of ropes. They slipped punches no one saw. When they threw punches, you couldn't tell if they'd made contact. What damage was done there. A broken jaw. A busted eye or lip.

It all required so much imagination.

When you got near a shadowboxer, the air around them felt different. It was like being on the inside of a bird's wing as it flies or tries to fly. These were the advanced students. They knew their stance and form. And it was beautiful just to watch them work. I wanted to be one of them, and I was. I got to be that.

I tell the pitcher's pal he can pull up a chair anywhere. He grabs one and sits by the window. He can see both outside and all of us with a slight move of the neck. He sits with his feet spread wide apart. Acts like he's packing something big down there.

I tell Noi, at the desk, to get the pitcher and his friend a bottle of water. Not the fizzy one. Makes him bloat.

I think of what to say to him.

I don't like to talk to people. The other girls are better at it than I am, and I don't mind nodding along. If I had a signature move, the nod is mine.

A quick nod when it's a yes to an instruction, to let them know I heard them. If they ask me if they should add something to their tab, I give three quick nods—an enthusiastic yes. The slower single nod, where I lift my chin and let it stay there for a while, means I am listening.

If it were up to me, I would just sit here, working. I just want to do my job and get them out. My job is in the details of their hands, toes, faces. Not their names or what they say to me. I can get so focused on a detail, on what's in front of me, in my hand, everything around me dims. I don't see the world outside that area.

I hate to say this now, but you know most people are not all that interesting. They're the same to me. Hands and toes, toes and hands. A lot of them say and think the same things. Predictable. And I have to behave like I never heard it before.

They all like to feel what they say is being listened to, and they all like to feel that they are the only person in the world who has ever had any feelings or had to deal with anything alone.

I file down a nail.

The pitcher asks me if I saw the game last night, and I tell him I didn't. He thinks everyone watches his games, and doesn't understand when he meets someone who doesn't.

Baseball is easy, if you ask me. You stand there in the sunshine and run around the field. A ball comes your way, you get under it. You get to be on television even if you're just sitting on the bench, or sitting there chewing gum or tobacco or sunflower seeds. And spit. It's never you alone, out there. You can have your moment. Hit a home run. Fill the bases. Strike them out. But you aren't alone.

No one goes out to see you hoping for your death.

"The guy sucks," I say, keeping my voice steady like I'm just talking about his nails. "Can't hit, can't run. It's why he's a pitcher. Can't even catch a fly ball. Catcher makes him look good. Pulling everything in."

He tells me to massage his thumb. I'll get to it when I do, but I don't tell him that.

"You think he's got a girl?" Mai asks.

"Probably a few he bangs," I say, because I know this type. I've been around guys like him at the gym. They talked freely in front of me because I was as good as them—no, I was better. When you're better than a man at something he doesn't think of you as a girl or about being a gentleman around you. How beautiful you are doesn't register with them. You quickly become their little sister, or one of the boys. I wasn't one of the girls who came into the gym not knowing how to wrap my hands. I came prepared. I knew how to throw a punch so they weren't going to teach that to me, and I couldn't pretend. Even when we were practising, the guys didn't want to spar. "Nah," they said, "I ain't stepping into that again."

"Nothing serious," I add. "Young like he is."

"What about that Elizabeth girl he mentioned last time," Mai says. She has a great memory. I don't know how she remembers, she just does like this.

"You remember that?"

"I was just thinking, you know," she says defensively, like I've accused her of something she wasn't supposed to be doing. "What she looks like and stuff."

I ask about Elizabeth.

He tells us she's a one-time thing.

A fastball to the head, a flying bat swung to the head, a broken finger, a slam, a fall, a miss. A trade. He can be a one-time thing too. He can't imagine that, though. He's that age where you don't think of the future. He lives only in the moment. Ten minutes from now is too far in the future for him to even imagine.

"You think he has any siblings?" Mai asks, wanting to know.

"Nah," I say. "Acts like he's the only one."

"You should tell him about Bob," Mai suggests, and laughs a little.

I think about it and decide not to. But then the pitcher asks me about him. He doesn't understand our language, but the name Bob he understood.

I tell him Bob is bobbing around. He laughs at my joke, and then asks if the guy is treating me right, as if he's a big brother checking in.

"Yeah," Mai says. "Is he treating you right?" She bounces her head from side to side and forces herself to smile.

6

I move up to his face.

Out of an old habit, I keep my eyes on the centre of his neck. From there, I can see everything else move. When I was in the ring, I always looked there. You could see the head, the shoulder, the hands, and what the feet were going to do. I knew where to punch, how often, to do the most damage. I didn't like to wait around to find out. I got them first.

The pitcher tells me he just wants his hands done today.

I tell him he should have us give him a treatment for his toes too. To prevent things. Being in the locker room barefoot with all those other guys. Who knows where their feet have been.

He thinks about it for a moment, and then agrees.

Mai works on his feet.

He doesn't ask me to work on his brows. I think of a reason to shape them. I tell him one of his eyebrows is a bit of a problem for him out there on the field. It's his tell. Once it lifts up a bit it means he's going to throw a curveball. This brow, I tap him there on the left, gives everything he's doing away.

He believes me, and I go to work.

"Is that true?" Noi asks. "I mean about the curveball."

"Hell if I know. I just made that stuff up so we can add up a bunch of things when he goes to pay."

"Get his whole face. Get the little hairs out of the way," Mai encourages, handing me the tweezers. "Tell him it's to keep sweat getting into his eyes out there. Toxins and oils." She adds, "Yeah. The one or two seconds he might need to blink it away could cost him a game. Or signal the wrong thing to his catcher."

I mention it, and he says to add that too.

He's already shaved his beard so I don't have to, and I can begin to thread his whole face. I get back to his brow. It seems I've taken off too much hair and accidentally made his right eyebrow higher than the left.

I worry he might notice this and reassure him. I tell him, this way when he's out on the mound, even as his brow is detailing his mechanics, in the distance it looks the same height as his left brow. Nothing to worry about. He can trust me, I tell him. And I work there for a few minutes, slowly, and try to fix it.

His pal gets up and stretches. Both hands above his

head join together and clasp. He sways side to side. Then he walks over to us and leans over my shoulder.

He's too close.

I see him from the corner of my eye, but stay focused on what's in front of me. He wants me to tell him about what I'm doing. A little bored, just sitting around. I try to bring him in to what we are doing, and say to him: When you control the centre line, you control the fight.

It's what Murch said to me all the time when we were at the gym. "You control the centre line, you control the fight! Centre line, centre line, centre line!" When I was too tired to think, he'd yell that. In the quiet of the dressing room before the fight, and after. Probably said that in his sleep too, to no one.

The man doesn't seem to know what I am talking about. Stares at me, two eyes blinking quickly back.

I didn't mean to give anything of myself away like that. I like to keep things about myself to myself. Keep my old life from mixing in with what I have now. It's better that way, not to let anyone know anything about you. It just came out of me like being touched on the part of the knee that kicks. Know where to poke and, despite trying not to—*kick*.

The man nods like I have given him a fact about my work, and I nod back, even though we don't understand each other.

I bow my head and keep working away. I don't see anything that isn't close to me. It's just Mai and her newly cut hair and me working.

The pitcher says something. His voice is light and flirtatious. He follows his question with a little laugh that says he's comfortable with us. That he can say this to us.

"—Oh my gosh," Mai says. "Tell me he didn't just ask for a 'happy ending.'" Mai has heard this stuff before, but she is always livid about it when someone says this to us. The pitcher jokes about it every time he comes in. Like I said, the guy thinks he's funny.

We are not all the same. It's fine if it is a place that wants to offer that. A person has to make their living, and you do what you have to. It's actually a kind service, too. But the way he laughs about it like we are just sitting here for him, stored in a cool, dry place, kept away from direct sunlight, waiting to be unrolled only one way, a little wet sac to stick himself into. The way he's so confident we want him and we are here to serve every which way, salivating, tongues hanging, lapping it up, begging. I resent how safe he feels sitting here in our space. Not scared of anything. It never occurs to him he could be killed with bare hands. He thinks he's perfectly safe, and the thing is, he's right. He is safe.

"We ought to take him to the back room," I suggest, joking. "Cut him up, you know."

Mai hands me a nail filer, and says, "Into pieces." She keeps her voice calm like she's just telling me what I should do to his nails.

At this point, Noi says: "And dump it. In different parts of the city." It's the first thing she's said that's her own idea. And it sounds funny because her voice is so soft it doesn't match with the violence of what she's just said. I am surprised at her enthusiasm too. When you look like everyone around you, and know the language, it's easy to fit right in, to feel comfortable to join.

"No one would know it's us, really," I continue, observing the girls. See how far we can take this. "They wouldn't even miss him. They can get some backup pitcher on the bench to fill in. Easy."

"Yeah," Mai agrees, and glances over at the other guy, "but there's his pal here. Gotta do something with him."

"Can't take down two, huh? Too messy."

A few minutes pass.

"Damn. Why's it never girls who ask for a 'happy ending'?" Mai asks. "I'd be more likely to give a girl a 'happy ending.'" Mai looks to the desk, waits for Noi to look over, and when she does, says, "What? A sister's got to look out for her girls."

When Mai and I are done with the pitcher, I watch him pay up at the register. When it gets to the tip, he waits awhile before deciding. Taps the first box, near the top of the screen—the lowest amount possible.

7

I feel a rush of air. I don't turn around.

I know Noi has got this—or at least she should get it. It's a walk-in. The woman wants a manicure. Noi, quickly remembering her line, tells her to pick a colour.

But the woman does not. Just stares at each of us, and lands her eyes on me. I know my line and say it. I remind Noi, "We have to say it twice like that. There's something about the second time we say it that it makes sense to them. They don't hear the first one."

The woman picks one colour. A pale pink. Same colour as the walls of this place.

A colour can be emotional. Pink is young, innocent, soft. Murch had insisted I wear pink when I was boxing. Wanted me to wear pink gloves and pink wraps and pink shorts.

"This is how you'll win. Pink," he said. "There's nothing these guys hate more than to lose to a girl. The minute they see this pink, they're going to think that they've got you beat, that it's going to be so easy. But no. It ain't that way. You got them beat. Now, you go in there and show them what's what."

Pink.

The woman sits down in one of the chairs lined up against the wall and tells us she has no plans for tonight. Just wants to get her nails done. Self-care, she says.

I don't like that term she uses. It's more like my-care. I'm the one sitting here, doing all the caring. The filing and the buffing and the polishing and the painting. The cleaning. It's all under my care.

Says she's tired.

"Like we don't know what being tired is," I say to Mai, grateful I can speak without Miss Self-Care understanding a thing.

I can tell she works in an office. The navy-blue suit, the fabric—it's a place that has air conditioning. The heels of her shoes aren't high. Enough to hear coming down the hall or turning the corner. All that she has on her is expensive. I can feel the clean.

"She just wants a manicure," Noi tells us.

"She better put that phone down, if she wants one," Mai says.

"What about her feet?" Noi asks, already thinking like she's worked here for a few months. "Can we add that, too?"

"Tell her combo. Two-for-one special. They don't want to do anything unless you use the word 'combo.'

They think they're getting a deal, a package deal, and they like that. And if she says it's too expensive just tell her 'Ten dollars.'"

Noi tells her about the combo and Miss Self-Care agrees. She goes to a pedicure seat, sits down, slips off her right shoe by putting pressure at the front of the shoe so the heel comes loose and it falls to the floor. With the left shoe she pulls it off with her right hand and arranges the shoes so they are close by. When she looks up, Mai is there with a tub of warm water and soap for her feet to soak in.

I let Mai concentrate. Let her look at the toes and what they need. Decide how much to cut, where to spend extra time polishing. When Mai has got to the point where she's moisturizing, I feel it's okay to ask her something.

I look at Miss Self-Care, and say to Mai, "What do you think her story is?"

Mai takes a few moments to observe, and then says, "Well, let's see." She shakes a nail polish bottle in her hand. Loosens the lid, and begins to paint. "Doesn't have a ring. Great skin. Loves her job. There's probably someone at work."

She paints the left big toenail.

"A young one. Twenty years younger. And they're in love," Mai adds as she quickly moves to the fourth toe. Miss Self-Care's toenails are tiny. They don't need that much polish. "He can't stand young women," she goes on. "They haven't got it together. They don't know what they want."

She moves to the other big toenail and says, "Probably owns her own home." Leans closer to me and says, "She gives him *self-care*," and she pauses here, and I know what's coming, "with her mouth!"

Self-Care asks us what's so funny.

Mai tells her it was an inside joke. Nothing she would understand.

Miss Self-Care's eyes stop squinting at us, and she brings them to our window. She looks at the traffic outside.

We don't take a Susan that can't speak our language. But it hasn't always been that way. One girl didn't know any other language than English. We were a little embarrassed for her about that. I mean, how were we supposed to talk shit about people with her? What if I didn't want to say something in English? To stoop to speak it to her so she understood?

She kind of picked up on a word we used often. We'd use it to describe her and some of our clients. We'd say it whenever she came in, or when someone like her came in.

We tried to teach her a few words. I tested her on her ability to say *dog* and *mother*. The words are similar, but she couldn't differentiate them in tone. I could just imagine the disaster she'd create. She'd say things like, "Well, isn't that cute, you carry your mother around with you.

She is so tiny, you can carry her around. Does your mother want a treat? A little treat. C'mon, c'mon. Let's get your mother a treat."

Of course, we had to be encouraging. Say things like, "Oh, you know how to speak our language," and smile. We're not supposed to make fun of them not knowing how to speak our language, that they only know about three words. We're supposed to be grateful they're even trying.

It isn't the same for us. Even after speaking the language for years, and *actually* knowing it, we still all get told with wide-eyed surprise our English is oh, just so good.

We had to go to the trouble of dyeing her hair black like ours, but she was so pale. It wasn't long before her roots started to show. Whenever I pointed out that her roots were showing, she'd tell me it was because her hair wasn't black like ours.

Well, she had a point there. She wasn't a lot of things we are. Now, whenever someone like her tries to work here—even if they're good—we just tell them they aren't the right fit.

I call over to Mai and ask if she remembers the girl, and give quick details of her.

Mai nods and says:

"Out of sight, out of mind. What's with you? Why are you even bringing her up right now?"

I want to say more, but pretend I don't care with a shrug.

Mai reminds me, "Just be glad she's not here anymore. Don't need to be doing my job and picking up someone else's job while they're here taking up space and getting paid to sit around."

"Remember when she got that Ken guy?" I ask.

She nods, and says bitterly, "The never-tipper."

"He tipped her, though," I say in a way like I want to be something I will never get to be for someone. "Didn't he?"

"Yeah. Walked right up to her and handed her the cash. Said she was his own kind," she says bitterly. "Like what are we, shit?"

I look at all of Mai's fingers working. And think of my nine. How I don't have all that she has and how I can't have all of it back. Mai, though, can have what I have in an instant. All she has to do is have the guts to do it. But I don't let myself think too long about it because Mai calls out in a cartoonish voice, "I don't know what to do with my extra time," pretending to be that girl.

I joke, pretending she is the girl who does not know our language, and say to her, "I don't pay you to sit around. You can clean the toilets."

She looks at me, then says, with fake innocence, "Clean? Doesn't it just do that itself?"

We laugh at Mai's acting.

After a few moments, she says angrily, "I'm the one who did the never-tipper's nails. It was like I wasn't even there. All he noticed was that girl. They had the same hair colour." After a few moments of thoughts I can't see, she asks, "Remember her lunch?"

"Bowl of maggots," I say.

"Damn," Mai laughs. "You gotta be so mean or what?"

I look out the window, at the door, the lock. I look at the space between us, and say, "Mac. Mac and cheese." I pretend to shudder, and make a face of disgust. "Can't believe anyone would eat that stuff. Maybe chew it, but to swallow that?"

"Gross," Noi says, joining us.

Mai stares at a space close to her. "Everyone thought she owned the place. They assumed. She gets to have that without having to do anything. The sight of her alone supposes she's boss. Bitch didn't even say who was boss. Just said she wasn't boss. Didn't point you out. And you're standing right there."

Rachel, my old boss, the one who taught me everything I know, wouldn't have had that. She'd walk over there and say, "He asked you who is the boss here. Who *is* boss?"

And she wouldn't leave it at that.

She'd tease it out longer. She'd ask, "Who pays you?" And wait. And shoot out questions so fast you wouldn't even know what was coming at you. "Who hired you? Who opens this shop? Who closes it? Who is the first person here before everyone else and the last to leave?

When there's a problem, who do you all come to? Who can fire you?"

But I'm not Rachel. I don't have her kind of courage.

The girl that didn't speak our language mostly sat here and read our magazines.

"What do you think she's doing right now?" Mai asks.

I stare outside at the cars on the street, and say, "Found work, probably."

"You think we're mean? Saying all this stuff about her?"

"Who cares. You think she'd stop and think twice about us? Probably tells everyone we all have sideways vaginas."

"What are you talking about?" Mai says, pretending. "Are you telling me all this time that we've known each other, you don't?"

8
—

My phone squirms in my pocket, and I take it out to look at its face. A few words and a red balloon is there. Mai notices and says to me, "Who is it?" I don't say anything, and pull the phone's face close to me and slip it down my side pocket. She knows when I don't answer that she should move on. And she does. She says, longingly, "We didn't book the pitcher's buddy."

"I don't think we could have got him."

"We don't know that. We never even offered."

"Just a feeling."

"You don't go on feeling," she says. "You ask. Ask, next time."

I don't say anything.

We're not in the ring. There isn't a fight, but Mai has a way of making it feel like there's one around the corner and I better be prepared. I don't meet up with Murch anymore, but it feels like he's been reborn through her. He occasionally sends texts or calls, wants to talk about old times. If it were still up to him he'd probably have me do road work. Have me out there pounding the pavement.

When Mai talks like that, I can hear Murch. Me and Mai, we are all about nails, but it's the same thing. It's still Murch there.

"You have to want to come out here and do this yourself," he insisted. "When you're in the ring and there's all that noise. Everyone's yelling at you to do something. 'Do this, do that. Jab, cross, hook.' You just remember they're on the sidelines. They ain't where you are. Don't let them get to you."

"We only had one walk-in," Mai says, like it's some kind of failure.

"Don't let it get to you," I say, "we'll get some more before the day ends." I turn to Noi. "Who's up next? Who've we got coming in."

I know who's coming in, but I want Noi to answer me as quick as I can see their name in my mind. But she clicks away at the computer. Then her eyes blink bright like an alarm. She tells me the screen is frozen. I tell her to check the book then. She opens a page, runs a finger down, stops, looks up, and says, "Alyssa."

"The waitress," I say, reminding myself, "at that restaurant around here."

"Which one?" Mai calls over. "There are so many on our street."

"The one with a swan painted on the window."

"They serve swan there or something?" Mai says, finishing up with the top coat. "It's false advertising, if they don't."

"They have good duck there."

Mai insists, coldly, "Duck ain't swan."

A few minutes go by, and then Noi asks me, "You ever gone to eat there?"

"A few times."

Noi and Mai look over at each other for a moment in silence. Any bit I say of myself that doesn't have to do with the shop gets sucked up by the girls.

I add, quickly, "—to support them."

"...with Bob, right?" Mai asks.

I don't respond to her, waiting for Noi to return her eyes to me. When she does, I say, "Their wait staff come here to get their nails done. We put them all on a tab, and the owner pays up at the end of the month."

Her eyes still looking over at us, Noi says, "Is it just her coming in? How come they don't all come together?"

"It's just her," I say. "Everyone has their own schedules."

"Alyssa," Mai repeats, remembering, "that the girl who likes to go on about her online dating?"

I nod.

Noi asks us, "Any of you ever done that?"

Mai smiles at Noi slowly and when the smile is wide enough it stays there and she turns to me, waiting.

"Why?" I say to Noi, like I have just swallowed a teaspoon of the water where Self-Care's toes were soaking. "Most of them are lying. They're married, have someone, or they've got a roster going... And what's happening in their own life that they can't find someone there? Why do they have to go online? I don't want the discards."

"People are busy. Maybe it hasn't worked out. They could be new in town," Noi lists, hopeful.

"Or hiding. You assume they are single because they tell you they are. But there's no one to ask to be sure," I say. I realize, too, that it's very specific, what I just said, like I know this from experience. But I don't think Noi catches on because she says, "Mai, how about you?"

"I've got my mother," she says flatly. "They all run the other way when they have to deal with that."

We laugh.

"You would get so many responses. Easy," Noi encourages, excited by the possibilities.

"Yeah," Mai agrees. "I'd probably crash the whole system."

It's been two weeks. The waitress's brows could use a cleanup. There are bits of hair on her eyelid. I wonder if she notices those bits. Most people don't. They don't look at their faces that closely. If it weren't for her boss, she'd probably not notice her chipped nail polish and maybe come in once every three months or so.

Mai sweeps and wipes down the centrepiece, puts away all our tools. Soap and lotion, water, towel.

I greet the waitress, and ask how she is.

I cringe at how I used to greet people. I used to just call out, "What do you want!" Their bodies stood very still, their eyes darted around, afraid to land on anything, and returned slowly back to me. They answered timidly, and in the form of a question, like, "A mani-pedi?" or "Just want to book an appointment?" Or they'd smile, and shrink their necks, say they'd come back another time. Sometimes they did come back, most of the time they didn't.

Mai told me I sounded bothered when I asked them what they wanted. I had no idea. I'd thought I sounded just fine. I mean they should tell me what they want. I can't read their minds. And it's out of the question to guess. Can't look at them and just tell them. It's rude, actually.

But you don't know how you come across to people unless they're honest and tell you. I appreciate that about Mai. She isn't scared of me. I didn't want to sound like that. Mai suggested I greet people with a question about themselves, let them take the lead. So I don't got to choose a topic.

The waitress says she's okay.

That could mean a lot of things. It's so vague. It's nothing I can work with. But she's not usually talkative at the beginning of the appointment. She's someone who needs to be drawn out. Then after, she takes over the show all on her own. Just work, look up and nod.

I let the moment pass.

Sometimes people come here for the quiet. We don't have the radio or any music playing. We like the quiet, and working in it. And just talking to each other, making each other laugh.

We do play music, though, when we want them to leave. Club music. Something with a lot of loud, meaningless beats—that feels like it's a headache. Like if it's been an hour and it's enough already, and we've told them their nails are dry, but they tell us they want to stay a bit longer to make sure.

Most of the time, when things are going great, we have no music. There's just the phone ringing and the clinking of our tools like inside a wristwatch. Quiet gears turning.

The waitress gives me her right hand. I bring the nail clipper to her thumb and cut. I watch the nail fall to the floor and it looks like a quarter moon. I look up and show her the length I have left behind and she nods approvingly.

She tells me about a guy she met online. A manager of something. She doesn't know what he does exactly, but he has his own house and two children. He was married for fifteen years. Really nice. Calls back. Drove out an hour to see her. She shows me a picture of him on her phone. I smile at it to be polite. And say to the girls, "The guy's hair is thinning."

Mai is the first to answer, "But is his money thinning?" She polishes our tools, turning a nail clipper to its back, and tries to see herself in it.

I bet the waitress is good at acting interested whether she cares or not. She probably does this by repeating what you just said to her, leaning in real close. I can imagine it right now. Her leaning in and being interested when there's nothing there. Her eyes big like her smile, teeth lined up end to end inside her mouth like a piano keyboard. I have seen her do this in the shop when a delivery guy came in once.

Mai says, "You don't have to talk a lot. You can just let your giggles flirt." She says this to me like I need this lesson learned. I bet you the waitress knows how to do this too, learned that from the job she has. She is encouraging when she giggles and it shows interest, not because it is actually funny.

That's dishonest, if you ask me. I mean how does it help them get better at being funny if you laugh when there's no funny there?

"But your face doesn't work that way," Mai says, looking at me with a little distance. "You make them earn it."

I think I've got too used to being by myself. I just don't care. It's nice, though. Not to care. Maybe people should try that sometime. Might be happier.

I ask the waitress if she thinks this one will work out.

"And money doesn't impress you," Mai continues, her head cocked to the side. "Because you've got your own."

The waitress says something, but I am not listening.

It sounds like what she said before and what she will say months from now. She thinks she's interesting because she goes on dates, and she gets them to go to bed with her, and they become her boyfriend, and then it ends. Abruptly. Never knows why. Ends up in my chair, going over the details, which I pull out like teeth.

"Oh, yeah," I say to the girls. "And. Then. What *happened*?"

The waitress doesn't know I am mimicking her. The way she is with people. Sometimes you show people how they come across and they can't even recognize themselves, laugh a little even.

I want her to talk more so I don't have to. Get her to believe I'm interested in what happens. Though I can't convince her to add more to the tab besides what her boss pays for her. Someone single and lonely can be made to want more from us. We can't tell her if she had red nails or shaped them round someone will be sure to ask her out. She's always got someone lined up.

I turn to Mai, who is wiping down my tools after pulling them from the blue liquid, setting them down one by one on the table to wipe dry. I say, trying to be helpful, "We need to get her with someone."

"Too bad, I don't have that problem," Mai says, sticking out her chest and leaning her back out. "They all want me."

"How come you ain't got anyone," I say, teasing, "if they all want you?"

She says quickly, "I know a guy for her." It is as if she's been lining them up somewhere just for this moment.

"What guy do you know."

"My dad," she says. "He's single."

We laugh because the man is as old as a raisin that fell underneath a fridge from eighty years ago.

"He doesn't know how to text, though," I say. "So I don't think it will work out for them."

I turn back to the waitress.

"Can you imagine this girl on a date?" I ask Mai. "She doesn't really have anything to say. Like a broken record. Don't you think, though, that sometimes the longing is better?"

"What do you mean?" Noi asks.

"I mean she loves talking about the beginning all the time, when they don't know each other. Same thing, each time. And then when it works, and she gets them, it's like what she really wanted was the longing."

"If we got her someone," Mai says, pondering, "she

wouldn't know what to do with him. He'd be nice. There's no drama in being nice. Might even call him boring."

I get to the waitress's left finger. Where a wedding ring would be, if she had one. This is the finger I don't have. And I spend time there massaging her knuckle, remembering what it was like to have this. I hold her finger and press into it, making a circle with my thumb, wishing a ring right there for her.

She looks down at my hand, and notices.

I don't hide what I don't have. I spread the space I do have wider. Pinky finger and middle finger go their separate ways. I know she wants to ask me about that. The missing finger. But she's too polite. It's not recent. I forget it's not there sometimes. And go about like it's still there. It's turned out to be a kind of superpower at work. For one thing, the finger is not in the way. There's more space to perch a client's toe or fingernail to paint. We don't get all tangled up with one another.

The waitress says something.

I ask her to repeat it. Once you zone out on someone, it can take a while to come back. It's like being underwater. A quiet hum, and then resurfacing. Learning how to take it all in and adjust to the new surrounding sounds.

She says she has her period and seeing all that blood makes her sad. It just means there's no life there, and reminds her she doesn't have anyone serious.

I don't add to that.

She says at work she sees people on date nights all the time. Their shining skin. The low whispers. She can tell who is in love and who isn't.

I ask her how she can tell.

People in love don't notice her. When she brings them food and drinks, or when she comes by to ask them if there's anything else they need. She might have to ask a few times.

She asks me if I can tell. At the nail salon. If someone's in love.

I think for a moment.

I guess I see them a lot here. Picking and grooming and wanting me to tell them they look good. Sometimes they just say it outright when I've got them in the chair. They just come right out and say it.

People in love are boring, if you want to know the truth. But I don't tell her that.

They are all the same. All love stories are the same. You meet, and that's it. Heartbreak can take years, splinting, cracking, flickering. The kinds of questions that form and turn back in on you before splitting out in all directions to explain why and how. Love doesn't have an explanation. Heartbreak, you don't need to prove. No one else has it and it always belongs to you. Forever yours. Love is actually not reliable. You have to depend on someone else to say they feel it too. And even when they do, you can't be inside to see the truth of that.

The waitress announces it is Wednesday. Stares at me blankly like I am not there. Just a board to bounce a thought off.

I want to say, "I know what we call this day of the week," but the way she says the word gives it so much meaning, like the other days don't exist.

I think she wants to say more, and I ask her about the crowd on Wednesday nights at the restaurant.

I think of moving to her toes.

Then I remember that her boss doesn't pay for pedicures because they can just wear a closed-toe shoe. It's the hands that are important, that they pay me for.

I look up and ask her if she'll get married if this guy is the one. I try to make sure it sounds like I am asking her this for the first time.

She says everyone wants a girl in her twenties. Men in their twenties, men in their forties and sixties. They all want them in their twenties.

I don't agree or disagree. I learned that a long time ago. That my opinion doesn't really matter. And the less I say, the more pleasant the memory of me today will be.

She tells me he texts her a lot. And smiles brightly like a child waiting to blow out candles on a birthday cake.

I bring over the nail colour she chose from our wall. It's clear. They don't like the serving staff wearing bright colours. Plain is the instruction.

She tells me about someone she used to go with. And he texts her too. Just her name. Three times. The waitress doesn't know what she's supposed to make of that. She wonders if it means he still loves her. Or thinks of her. Or misses her. Wants to get back together. Is with someone.

It's probably all those things, I say.

I look at the finger I don't have. I'm actually quite proud of it and want to hold it up any time someone sits in my chair. If my body has a centrepiece, it's this space where something used to be.

9
—

Back here, I can hear a group of women trickle in. Filling the salon floor with giggles and voices. I can't see their faces and don't know how many there are, but I can tell by the sound there's probably more than three. When there are two it's quieter, because when one speaks they know the other is listening. There is a third person there because whoever talks has someone echoing it with encouraging *yeah*s and laughs. When I go out to the front room, I panic because I have trouble with this group instantly.

I can't tell any of them apart.

I am good at my job and this usually comes easy to me, but damn, they each have the same outfit on. A white cotton dress and cream-coloured flip-flops. They aren't all related. They are friends.

One says she's Liz-ee with a *y*.

The other one says she's Liz-ee with an *ie*.

Lily.

Lou.

Mai asks me: "Tell me if it's just me, but can you tell these girls apart?" When I don't seem to be paying attention, she snaps, "You paying attention?"

I say to her, "We don't need to tell them apart. Just get them done and out. They want everything done. Toes, nails, face, hair." I look at those parts quickly—toes, nails, face—and quickly try to find differences among them. Shapes, textures. Gait, voice, manner.

I knew we needed an extra girl on the floor with us. I have Nok down for this shift, but it's been half an hour already and she's still a no-show. Hasn't been in when she's scheduled or come in at all. The new girl can't do nails yet. As if hearing the voice thinking inside my head, I hear Mai say from the desk: "It's been a half hour and Nok's not even here. Why keep scheduling a no-show?" She pauses. "If that were me, you'd tell me I was out and not to come back."

"Just talk to these girls and tell them to pick a colour. By the time they've done all that it will be fifteen minutes in."

I try Annie's phone. Ask her to get here in ten minutes.

Mai talks to the bridal shower, but calls over to me, "You still holding out for Nok or are you done with her?"

"She's going through some stuff," I say, looking at the bridal group in front of us. Still looking for their differences.

"You want me to go by her place after my shift? Just to check?" Mai asks.

"I can do that."

"You don't have to do everything yourself."

"I can do it."

I think back to what happened two weeks ago.

"You up for giving me a few months' pay now?" Nok had asked me.

"That's a lot all at once," I said, hesitating.

"I know," she agreed. "It's just I'm short. Running behind on bills."

Her ex hadn't kept up his payments. Threatened bankruptcy. If he went through with it, that would be it. None at all. So I gave it to her. Wrote out a cheque. And she hasn't been in since then.

I remember her first day here.

Nok came in with her kids. Those two little ones. Seven and five, girl and boy. She had no place to drop them off. No family to look after them. It was only going to be the one time.

We had suggested they stay in the back room with crayons and paper, but after only two minutes they ran out to the front.

They wanted to see their mother.

Children know how to get attention. Just them sitting there by the window had people looking in and waving. The little boy walked up to the window and put up both hands, patting the glass. He'd put one hand in the air and a passerby would stop, give him a high five. And then he'd wriggle from side to side. The girl joined him and did the same.

I never threw out their drawings.

Then Nok just started to come in with the two of them for her shifts all the time. It just kind of happened, and I didn't say anything about it. They didn't have a place to go. Besides, I liked having them around. I haven't got family. But when I think about it, I have what I want to have. Does me no good to say that, though.

I told those kids about the aquarium. You can touch a stingray.

"Scary!" the boy said.

"Won't it sting you?" the girl asked.

"I wouldn't be scared," I said bravely. "They remove the stinger so it's safe."

"They shouldn't remove it," the boy suggested. "They should invent a device and ... and ... and attach it ... to the end so it doesn't sting you."

Kids. They come up with ideas just like that. No one's told them "That's not how it works," "That can never happen," or "How is that possible?" I thought it, but I didn't say. Didn't want to be one of those voices.

When we weren't busy, they liked putting makeup on me and the girls. We'd line up in a row, and they'd pick up a brush and colour in our eyelids, make circles on our cheeks, and line our lips.

"—Hey, she's here," Mai tells me.

It's the standby girl, Annie. Took her about ten minutes. She pulls at the glass door and enters the shop. Waves to everyone in one swoop. She is wearing a pink summer dress, and I eye that. She knows what I'm thinking and says, "Yeah, I have my clothes," taps her tote bag, and slips away.

The girl's name—Annie—doesn't mean anything in our language. She would be thought of as beautiful, but she slouches. She is a little taller than the rest of us at the shop, but standing near us with that slouch her height doesn't get noticed at all. Doesn't help that whenever I look over at her she always finds something to stand behind—it's either me, or the other girls, or a client, a desk, the centrepiece.

"Susan," Annie says to me, looking at my name tag with a smirk. She looks over at Mai and says again, "Susan."

"Susan," Mai echoes.

"Ladies, ladies, ladies. Are we fully booked, or what?" I say excitedly to all the girls on the floor. "Business is *boom*ing!" I shout like a circus host.

We laugh to ourselves. Our names popping like the bubbles in the plastic tub we bring to our clients.

Lizzy, Lizzie, Lily, Lou. Lizzy is the bride, not Lizzie. To make things more difficult for us, Lily and Lou are actually identical twins. I am the first to move and take Lizzy to the wall and point to the water for her toes. And she knows what to do.

Mai takes Lizzie.

Lou and Lily tell each other to go first, have Annie take them. After their fussing, Annie takes one.

Lizzy is the first to talk.

She asks who is getting married. She knows the answer, but she just wants it said out loud. She wants a cheerleading squad. Her bridesmaids all yell out her name and the Susans join in too.

I don't know why I don't join.

I look over at Lizzie and wonder if she might, for a moment, think it's her, since her name sounds exactly like the bride's name. She gives no sign and I know they can tell themselves apart easily because they all know each other.

Lizzy has decided they will all wear the same colour polish. A light pink.

We will start with their toes because polish on the toes takes longer to dry and gets ruined easily. Then, we'll move to their hands. After that, threading and tweezing.

Lizzy tells me she doesn't want wax on her skin. She feels threading is more precise because you measure the angle of the face better with a thread.

I agree with her, but I want her to feel I am giving her what she wants. When you agree with someone they don't notice you. I talk a bit about waxing, how the warmth feels good on your skin and opens the pore around the hair root, relaxes you naturally so when we do pull out the hair there's less irritation. I put up a bit of resistance to make her feel like I am not going to do a thread so when I agree she feels relieved and reassured that I'm on her side.

When I am done painting, I will pass the bottle to Mai. Then it will go to Annie. By the time Mai passes it back to me, I will have Lizzy's hands ready to paint.

Once we have them in a chair like this, we don't move them around. They are getting everything done. Takes too much time for them to move, to go where we want them to go. Moving them is a risk. Might trip, nail colour hasn't dried, and we'd have to start with all that again. In and out, in and out is all I'm thinking of doing.

It takes a lot to focus and paint. The paint starts at just a little distance from the cuticle. Needs that room so it grows out nicely. Not having that distance is poor technique. Don't want to have poor technique. I look at the nail and its shape. How much of the finger or toe the nail takes up. Can't put a big blob of paint. Takes longer to dry that way and air might slip underneath. Might form a bubble in a few days. Plus, I can't be generous. Adds up, you know.

Lizzy, I notice, has a mole the size of a small pebble underneath her big toe. I feel relieved. It's like seeing the shore from a distance. A place to land. It's a spot where you know that this belongs to this person and no other here.

I am always looking for the thing that makes people different from each other. Most people want to belong, to look like someone they've seen, to be like other people. I don't. I like the distance, and the thinking I do from there.

I look over at her friends—Lizzie, Lily, Lou—and turn back to Lizzy, look for what else on her makes her different.

There is a skin tag near her wrist. There are a few batches of hair on each of her big toes. She should shave them, but I don't think she's noticed them. That's an area a lot of people don't think of shaving. Might also be that she's near-sighted. Her third toe on her left foot is longer than her big toe. Just slightly. Huh. There might have been an eleventh toe. I feel a nub of something there like it's missing, and I see a healed scar. Some people have more than they really need.

I don't ask about that.

She doesn't notice my finger. To notice that, you have to be looking at me. Since she's come in she hasn't really looked at me. She knows I am there and what I do. She knows that of the other girls too. She knows the nail colour she wants, her friends, where to sit, where to pay. She even notices the street outside. The time.

But not me.

I don't mind. I would have to talk about myself, what my life is like outside of here. Family, friends. Don't want to talk about any of it. Just want to work. When she looks at the top of my head when I am painting, I lower it. If I look up, she might try to get us talking. This way, her need to talk is directed at her own friends—who she knows.

I touch the heel of her foot and she squiggles it away. Means she's ticklish there. There's a laugh, but it doesn't come from Lizzy.

My ear finds the laughter.

It's Lizzie. Her big toe is what makes her laugh. When Mai reaches for it, she pulls it back instinctively, and apologizes. Then brings it back, bracing.

Lou has freckles on her legs. She likes the yellow nail polish, but wants to look like the rest of the party. She stares longingly at the yellow nail polish bottle. She won't wear it, but she asks Annie to test it so she can see what it looks like on her.

When Annie is finished painting her left pinky—that's the nail I like to demonstrate on, too, because it's small and uses up less nail polish—Lou tells her maybe it's a colour for next time.

We move on to the threading.

Lizzy has two beauty marks at different spots in her eyebrow. They are very small. I doubt she notices, or that anyone looking at her would notice. There's also another tiny beauty mark on her chin.

Beauty marks have meaning to us Susans. We read them like tarot cards. One near the lip means you're a talker. One on the eyelid means you will spend a lot of time sleeping in this life because to see it the eyelid has to be closed. One near the tear duct either means you will make other people cry about you or you will cry about other people. Sometimes you're born with a beauty mark, other times they just appear suddenly. I know someone who got hers removed, but a few years later it appeared on her son's face. You can't escape them. They reveal things about you to us whether you want us to know or not, and we know what's destined for you.

At my right, Mai is working in sync with me. It is like we are one. Measuring and pulling the same areas of hair. I wonder what she's noticing. What particulars stand out. I want to go over there, stand near her, see what she sees, feel her work. But I have got my own work in front of me.

I quickly glance over at Annie, and she's steps behind. Still on the toes. She should have moved to hands, and like us, be at the face doing something about the hairs. Might have to join her, help her move along.

I will get to Lily in no time. Or is that Lou? I don't know and decide it's Lily sitting there at the station. I glance at her and her two thumbs tap dance on the screen of her phone. I look at her toes and see how long her toenails are. I won't ask her if she wants them cut or filed. I will just offer to cut them.

They all get what they ask for, but I do the work of asking leading questions that get them to ask for what they should have done. I know what they should get done, the way those lawyers with fancy suits on television already know the answers of someone on the stand. I draw it out, what I already know the answer to. I draw it out.

I ask if Lily wants her toenails cut.

Lily, sitting above me and peering down at her toes, tells me they look short to her already.

They do, from where you are sitting, I want to say, but they are not.

Instead I offer to cut. I bring the tip of my left thumb and the fingertip next to it together and show her how little I want to cut.

She doesn't notice the missing finger. Just the space I have made with the ones I do have.

She nods.

I nod too, and cut the toenail. I watch the bit I cut fall to the floor. I cut nine more quarter moons from her.

I perch some of her toes where my missing finger is. It's a good thing to have all this space. I can move quickly, get them in and out. And they don't know how I am able to do that.

Lily has a patch of dry skin on her right knee. She's scratched at it several times it's almost red. I bring an ointment from my basket and rub it in.

On her left inner leg there's a line of hair she's missed. Means she shaves with a razor and was in a rush to be done. Maybe she got soap in her eye and couldn't see through the hail from the shower and forgot about it.

She is not ticklish.

Her hands are strong like she works with them all day. I ask her what she does, and she says she's a receptionist.

Someone who types all day at the desk has a lot of tension between their fingers. I spend extra time putting pressure there, and also on her knuckles and the area that allows the thumb to spread. Every time I move to another finger to put on a nail colour, she resists, and I remind her to relax.

Noi, observing this whole time, brings out bottles of water and hands them to each. I tell Lily I have placed hers on the chair.

I move over to Lou, still with Annie, and file down her thumbnail. It was a short nail. It opens up the skin and splits. Blood rushes out.

I apologize.

Annie looks on, surprised I would make such a rookie mistake. I pretend I'm not bothered and grab alcohol and something to seal it.

Lou winces.

I catch, out the corner of my eye, Lizzy looking at the park across the street. I turn my whole head to her, and she seems to look further than that. I can see her mind turning and thinking as her eyes are fixed on that distance.

It's the face of someone who is thinking of the future, the rest of their life. I see the shape of her eyes change. They look larger, but they are not. It's tears. When that happens you don't ask someone what's wrong, unless they say. I leave my noticing and turn back to Lou.

I thought the floor would sound like it does before a big fight. Everyone yelling to get pumped up for the big moment. Murch used to say to me, "Ain't nothing to be scared of. You walk in there, in that ring, you already won. You already won by being there." I think of saying that, give some sort of wisdom about life, but it wouldn't make any sense to anyone but me. It's a strange quiet. I can hear what is outside. A streetcar. The warm and long honk that can only come from a truck.

The phone rings.

I feel my heart beat in my chest like there's a pigeon pecking at me from the inside. I know someone out there wants me.

10

Annie got her start at Bird and Spa salon. That's the place Rachel owns, where I used to work.

What kind of name is that anyway—Bird and Spa salon? I wouldn't know it had to do with nails. I'd have thought it was for parrots or someplace you brought birds and pets to. Some grooming place. Wouldn't be far off, too, if you want to know the truth.

My old boss there liked you best if you could just be a parrot. Watch what she does, say what she says, and repeat and repeat. Don't try to be your own person. She'll stomp that out of you.

Rachel has a brother named Raymond. They call her Ray, though. And together, that brother and sister are called Ray-Ray. They were always around each other. Rachel had a way of making you want to be like her. To want her respect and love. The kind of big sister, if she had your back, you just felt safe in the world.

Raymond had that safety. Even if he didn't want it, he

had that. It was by blood. He didn't have to earn it like the rest of us. Even if we came close, it couldn't be like they were. Sure, she could make you feel like you were family. But get a job somewhere else, strike out on your own, she'd never heard of you. You didn't exist to her.

Mai says that's all in the past. Forget and forgive. Easy for her to say. She never worked there.

"You don't need them," she's often reminded me.

I hate to want anything. And wanting to be liked is the worst. Depending on another person to give, to be kind.

"You got your own place now."

"Yeah, but I got to do everything myself."

I realize that's not true, but I don't apologize, and Mai doesn't ask me to.

"Better that way," she says.

Family. Blood is what they are. Still linked and together. You're supposed to leave home. Supposed to make it without family.

I did.

I've got more balls than Raymond does, if you want to know the truth. The way he makes himself smaller around his sister, tucking in all his sides like he's one of those little potato bugs. Does whatever his sister tells him to do. No questions asked. That sucker.

But damn, he sure can draw those little designs on

someone's nail bed. We don't do any of that stuff here. Just the basics. In and out, in and out.

Anyway, many of the girls I've taken in here got their start over there. They all start a little jumpy and shaken even at the slightest thing. Anyone enters the shop and they freeze for a bit and have to shake themselves out of it.

I have to remind them they aren't there anymore. It's safe. The phone rings. They jump. Stare at it for a bit like it's got a living life and is about to explode, reach tentatively for it before suddenly realizing it didn't go off and they can just settle down now to answer it. They have to talk themselves out of the place they've been before.

Rachel did that to my girls. Always spitting out some criticism, knocking things over when she's upset. Making a scene. She did that to me, too. She can't just tell you how to do something. She's got to yell it and make it personal. And dig, and rub.

If I was slow, she'd yell, "What's with you today? Got your head knocked around?" If I was a little late to my shift, she'd say, "What's with your legs today? Open them so wide last night you can't walk fast enough this morning?" She had to act this out to you too, lowering herself to the floor and spreading her legs—and she did this in front of the clients. They'd look on, not sure what to do, or worse, amused.

And so what if I did? That was my business. How was it any of hers?

Of course, I kept those comments to myself. Sticking up for yourself, explaining, that just keeps her going. She loves an audience, and I didn't want to give her anything that would feed it.

This one time, she said to me, "What's with your face today? Do I got to dig out your nose?" So much for sisterhood. We have the same nose shape. Just because we look like each other or come from the same place doesn't make us family. We don't *all* get along.

"I look out for one person," she'd say. "And that's me. I'm not your sister. Not your mother. Not family. The sooner you know that, the better it will be for us. You work here, on that floor, and you're on your own. I ain't gonna save you. A client upset? That's on you. You take care of it. Don't know what to do out there? I'm not gonna come running by and do it for you or show you how."

Except for her brother Raymond, of course.

He acts all helpless and like things are so hard for him, but if he ever told you about his tips you wouldn't believe his act for one second. And you wouldn't spend any time on pitying the guy. He knows exactly what he's doing. Knows exactly. He's playing everybody.

And oh, if you just happened to look at her brother, Rachel would say, "No, no. No look. Raymond is expensive," and she'd go over and fix his shirt which she insists he wear in a size too small for him to show off his body. And that dumb chunk of muscle grins, too.

I know her.

She says and does things like that so we don't forget. Like am I ever going to forget what I learned the days she said each of those things to me? Even today, my cheeks blow up red thinking of what she's said to me.

When I'm slow in the shop, her little voice comes into my head to hurry me up. "Why so slow today? Did the thing he throw into you last night, was it too big for you?" She would give a couple of shoves to go along with that. Show you exactly what she meant if you didn't get it.

I can hear her in my ear when I'm yelling at one of the girls. I know I shouldn't. It's not even me to talk like that. Just comes out that way. Thing is, it's contagious or something. I want to talk to the girls that way, too, but that's not me. Like when the girls use the washroom often. If that happened at Bird and Spa salon, Rachel would say, "Did you drop one in there? You didn't wipe yourself good, did you? Can smell that from here, girl." She would reach behind her and fan.

That girl knew how to shame you.

She read you like she'd known you your whole life. She'd look and pause and be amused and come out with one of her questions. And she'd make them no longer than two sentences.

But damn. Hate or love her, that girl could make you laugh. She was great at doing impressions. She'd pick a few things to exaggerate about a client and act it out for you when there was a lull in the day.

"Who's this? Guess who this is?"

She'd sit in a client chair and stick out her toe, and say something like, "Hey bitch. Why don't you take care of this ingrown toenail. You know I can't do it myself. Oh, now, don't you worry about that yellow stuff at the bottom of my feet. Just slice off the dry skin like a pat of butter. You know you want me. Ain't ever washed my feet, but you know you want me."

We knew who it was without her having to say.

"Oh my," she'd say, flopping down at a station and lifting a hand to her forehead like she had a hot fever and leaning into her *r*'s real hard, "I just don't know how we are going to make it. With the private school tuition, ballet and piano, our cottage out on the beachfront, our trip to Hawaii which we take every year, and our nanny, and our three cars—" she'd press a palm to her chest and finish with, "We're just *really* struggling."

We knew who that was, too. We'd had all of them in more or less the same form sitting in front of us. Paying for our mani and pedi, our combos, colours, and time.

Raymond's like his sister. They come from the same place. I know some of the Susans here have been with him. Some admit it, some won't ever. It's my feeling that Raymond's plugged them all. But like I said, that's not my business.

11

I look outside.

The sandwich board isn't there. It's everything to us. Tells people who we are and what we do in here before we get to say ourselves. Tells anyone what we offer and how much better we offer it. Not having it out there is a loss. Without it, we can't compete. Without it, it's like not showing up.

I grab the sandwich board with one arm and take it out myself, split open the board on the sidewalk. I push the board from the side to see if it will fall over. Don't know why I didn't think to do this earlier. I'm a creature of habit. Maybe I was knocked out of my routine talking to the new girl and telling her about how things work around here.

You can't just put a sign out here because you feel like it. A few weeks ago, I had to renew a permit to put this thing out. I look down at the scrawl that is my handwriting written with pink chalk. Maybe this might get them to book an appointment, might get us more walk-ins. Got to keep things moving in and out, in and out. Twenty minutes max.

I go back inside.

I don't have to be outside or hear a weather report to know it's summer. No one's got to tell me that. I can feel it in the shop when I'm near the window. I can just look at the appointment log, see how filled up that thing is. Best season for us. Everyone wants to show their nails. Get something done before they go on vacation. I can tell from their shoes, all those toes poking out, or when I've got a foot in my hand. All bundled up for months. Cracked, dull nails, dry heels.

It'll be lunch soon.

When there is time for lunch, I usually tell the girls to take it and I watch the front desk myself. When they come back, we move on to the rest of our appointments. I take my lunch at the end of the day, which is dinner for everyone else.

I watch the clock.

The parking spot in front of our window opened up some time ago. I didn't notice a car had pulled out. But I notice the car pulling in. That sand-coloured pickup truck.

Murch has one like that.

Murch should be retired now. Still thinks he's got a big shot, coaching that new itty-bitty for the Olympics. Murch.

The name sounds like a grunt. My guess is he's a bit over two hundred pounds now. His skin sags and drips like an old candle with drooped wax all around its sides.

I still remember my fights. There was this one. The girl had long arms. Murch said I could take her out in four. He said, "Four rounds max. She'll be tired. Long-armers, if they make contact, don't let you get close. Find a way to get inside. Slip quickly and get her ribs on one side and then when she nurses that one side get her on the other side. Bam, bam." He punched the air on one side and then on the other. Showing me. Like I forgot what that looked like.

I looked at the girl. She took wide steps, too. Long legs. And she stood close to the ropes. Both gloves far from her face. I could use that. Jab close and her own gloves would hit her face. Jab. Ooomph. Murch said she was a bleeder.

Get in close. Make it uncomfortable for her. It will make her move around, away from the ropes. When you land one, drag your glove a little. Blood is good here. We weren't far in and she was out of breath. Nerves do that to you.

I threw out three jabs. First one by her temple. Then neck. Then ear. Her ear was clean. Perfectly shaped. When she threw a jab, her shoulder didn't come up to protect it. That's how you know she's not good. I could shape her ear.

I threw a left hook. Slam. She came forward. I got her to move away from the ropes. She was breathing in gasps of three quick breaths. Sweat dripping. Jab. Dragged my glove. I didn't take my eye off the centre of her neck. I shuffled.

She looked at my feet when I shuffled. And I hung back. I let her throw one at me and I slipped it.

She had a tell. She looked at a spot before it landed. Her eyes went there first. I met her at every throw. Knocked what she gave me away. Before she went back into position, I threw a jab at her temple. Flick. A gash opened up by her right eye. Red.

All that was a long time ago. Susan's. The girls. I've got this right now. When you're good at your job, doesn't matter what it is, you just feel good about your corner of the world. I get to have a place to come to every day.

If Murch walked in he'd probably be wearing shorts, but he shouldn't. It's the shape of his legs. They look like frogs, thin little things. It's like all that food he takes in keeps filling up his middle but never makes its way down to his legs.

He'd wear sandals, too. No matter the season. And they would have Velcro. What's a grown man doing with Velcro? It's for kids who don't know how to tie their shoes yet.

I made a point of telling him that he shouldn't wear shoes with Velcro and he belly-laughed and said, "I ain't got what little time I have left tightening and looping a little itty-bitty shoelace into a knot. This is one pull. Bam. Just makes life easier. Don't you think life ought to be made easier if it could be? C'mon, lay off me, will you?"

I bring my mind back to the shop, and say to Noi, "You got the list for me?" She doesn't know what I mean and Mai explains, "Supply list. Top drawer."

She hands it over and I look down at the items.

"I thought I just bought a bunch of reds. I thought we were just offering twenty? What's this new orange-red you have here?" I ask, accusingly.

Noi begins to mouth something, thinking she should be explaining something she doesn't know anything about.

"—The clients want it," Mai says, cutting in. "It's summer, and it looks good."

I go further down the list.

"And what's this grey-blue colour. It makes a person look like they are the walking dead."

"Try telling that to them."

We laugh, knowing that we never tell clients what we really think. Then Mai comes closer and says to me quietly, "How's that shoulder?" She reaches toward it, but I step away, and say quickly, "It's fine."

I don't want Noi to know anything about my shoulder. Then she might ask about it too. I don't like for them to worry about me. It's too close.

Mai, though, doesn't let it go, and says, "Still bugging you?"

"I said it's fine."

"Didn't come back before it healed, did you?"

"I'm good."

She treats me like some pigeon with a broken wing. A prized pigeon.

The phone in my pocket jiggles and I pull it out to see who it is. A few words pop up. Before I read what it says, I drop it into my back pocket.

I don't have to read what Murch types, I can hear his voice in my head. "You know how to take a punch. Just lean into it. You just take it. That'll scare the shit out of them, to see you still standing. You got this, Ning."

Ning.

It's the name people call me when I'm not at Susan's. I've been here so long my old name feels like it belongs to someone else. It means tickle in our language. It is a single sound. The beginning sounds a lot like its ending, but the ending is different because of how it closes out the sound. So final. You barely have to open your mouth to say it. You could even say it with a jaw wired shut.

I haven't heard anyone call me that name in what feels like decades.

Mai usually says "Hey" and whatever she needs to say. She rarely ever says my name. I don't want to be anything other than Susan.

12

There's a lull in the shop and I don't like the quiet. Too much time to think and not do. I stand by the door, watching. From the corner of my eye, I see Mai come toward me from the centrepiece. She asks me, "Everything okay with you?"

I shrug.

"Your phone has been buzzing a lot. Who is it?"

"No one."

"You don't got to tell me that," she says, like I've betrayed her. "It's someone."

"My mom," I quickly say. I don't have to explain about that. She knows. "Wants money. It's all I'm good for to her."

She doesn't push me to say more. She's got mom stuff too. Her mother has no place to go. Most children move out of the house, try to make it on their own—and they can because their parents can take care of themselves. But Mai's mother isn't like that. She's been taking care of her mother because that's what's expected. Some people have children so they have someone to take care of them. Better than getting a job, hiring a nurse. A lifetime of service paid with guilt. It is fine when you are mewling and puking, but you get to be an adult and it's prime time to provide. Mai does that. She provides. I don't, though. With my mom, whatever I give, it's never enough. She comes back to drain it all.

We leave it at that. I change the subject and move on. I ask, "Who's next?"

"Marla."

She's a regular. I walk over to prepare at my station, the one closest to the door, but I don't have to do a thing. Mai thought of it earlier, I guess. The basket is there, the lotions and oils turned with the pumps facing me.

I look at the clock again.

Marla's probably looking for a parking spot. She gets off work early.

Mai reminds me, "Don't forget to tell her something about Bob. You told her last time about Bob." She thinks about something for a moment, and then says, "You didn't mention Bob with the wedding girls. Been wanting to hear what you're going to come up with." She lightly touches me on the arm.

And I let her.

I can feel the black hairs on my arms part at the spot she landed and when she pulls away there's a slight warmth there. I remember I am alive and I have a body, and that it wants things.

"No reason," I say, and touch where Mai did, "to bring him up so much."

"—What?" Noi's voice interrupts us, asks, "Who's Bob?"

"A tool," I say.

Noi's curious and alert face softens into something else, like I've just thrown an object at her. She wanted to get to know me, and I didn't open up to her. I feel bad about that, and give a little more. "I've got ninety-nine problems and let's just say Bob's a bitch that ain't one."

Noi looks over at Mai, hoping she can provide what I don't.

Mai says, "Her man."

"Oh, I didn't know you had someone."

"Why wouldn't she?"

"She seems," and Noi looks over at me before darting her eyes back to Mai, "like she doesn't need anyone."

Mai laughs, and says to me, "The girl's right, you know. Only worked with you for one day and knows this about you already." She turns back to Noi and says, "Bob's cool. He's one of us."

"How did you and Bob meet?" Noi asks me.

"Yeah," Mai picks up, "how *did* you meet? You going to tell us that? Huh?"

I think of something and say, looking across the street at the park bench, "It was there." I push my chin up and point with it. "On that park bench."

"He was barefoot, right?" Mai's eyebrows jump up and down, egging me on.

"Yeah," I say, playing along, "and I sure thought his toes were real good-looking."

"And his teeth. What did you think of those?" Mai asks, over at the desk now and leaning close to Noi. "She has a thing about teeth. Loves them."

"Like little Chiclets."

"And, uh, ah-ha," Mai says, "what about that growth on his back? That bump with little bits of hair that he calls his twin brother. Baby Bob back there."

We laugh.

Noi looks at Mai and then at me, and says sadly, "You don't got to make fun of me." She turns to the computer screen and says to it, "I just want people to have someone. If that's what they want."

When she says that, I begin to feel my age. People still look at me, and I can get them to look at me, but my openness is closing up.

I've heard just about every kind of problem possible. I don't have to experience it myself. My clients are in my chair every day. Either at the centrepiece, the stations, or along the wall. Telling me about experiences I haven't had or lived. All of them true. I don't need to live them or experience them. Universe, I say, I hear you through them, and I have learned my lesson.

"We're not making fun of you," Mai says to Noi, tenderly. "We're just having fun."

"Bob's not real. Just someone I bring up once in a while," I say, with a shrug, "to fill out a conversation."

Noi looks at my face and then looks steadily at a space on the ground between us. She wants to say something to me. She's young, so she's hopeful about people. That they are for the most part good. But it's hard to say that out loud to someone you don't really know.

Bob.

What a name, huh? It's a name made up of a bunch of circles that go nowhere but into itself. A name someone can remember, and also forget. A name with letters that look like boobs, or eyes, or an open mouth. Like something a child draws up to colour in later.

I say to Noi, "I make all kinds of shit up about Bob. Depending on my mood. I see text messages pop up on his phone from people I've never met before. He comes home late. He drinks a bit too much. Bob delivers food. He's a janitor. He drives a truck. Clients like it when you've got some man to complain about."

"Does it work?"

"Keeps them off my back."

"Seems like a lot of stuff to remember each time."

"They don't know what to make of a woman alone, and content. Weird, they say. It's how people think."

I bring a hand up to my ear and place my fingertips just underneath the lobe and ask, "You hear that?"

No one says anything.

"Yeah," I say, nodding my head enthusiastically. "It's called peace."

I continue, "Bob. Crap like that." I look away from Noi. She hangs on my every word and I am embarrassed for her that she wants to know me so much. I look out at the passing cars and say, "Fucking pick a colour already, you're in my world."

We are all soundless in the shop, if you were looking at us from the outside.

"I'm doomed, aren't I?" I ask Mai, letting her know more about me than I wanted her to. "Going on about this Bob. Seems more interesting and fun than anyone real."

"You're just afraid of love," she says, kindly, and without any judgment or offer to change and fix. "That's all."

After a moment, Mai says, "Well, I got a Bob story you could use," her voice anticipating something fun. "He got someone else pregnant after telling you for years he didn't want to have children."

"Doesn't sound tragic," I say.

Noi offers something else: "He got someone else

pregnant and there was a miscarriage. And instead of flushing it down the toilet, he puts it in a glass jar."

I don't know where Noi got that from. But I play along. "And I thought it was pickle and cooked it up?"

"Oh, man," Mai says, delighted Noi has thought of something original for Bob to do. "But that's too original. How about—"

I cut in.

"It's gross," I say, disgusted at what I came up with so easily.

"How about," Mai says, picking up what Noi started, "it just sits in a jar in your kitchen?"

"Why would it be there?" I ask.

"So he can see it every day."

"Sounds too weird. No one is going to believe that."

"How about he buries it in your backyard. In a glass jar?"

"And what?"

"And every year you two dig it up on its birthday and get it a cake and blow out candles."

"It's too weird. Relatable is the goal," I instruct. "Not off-putting."

"What's wrong with that? You and Bob are weird. There can be weird people. I mean pulling hair off someone's face is weird. So is a shop that just paints people's nails. And everyone's name is Susan."

"Remind me," I say to Mai. "What did I tell her about him last time?"

"Hawaii," she says, thinking, and keeping it short. "He got stung by a jellyfish."

"Did I say what he does for a living?"

"Teaches."

"What does he teach?"

"Math. You always say he teaches math."

Right. Math. Numbers and equations. At the local high school. Been there for a long time. Loves it. His students adore him.

"Did I say anything about kids?"

"None."

"You sure?"

"I remember. You said you worried he might take off with one of the teachers at the school. Someone younger."

"Is that right?" I ask, amused at my own ability to just make things up as the day goes along or the moment calls for it.

"Yup. I thought it was funny," she cackles. "Your face. You were so serious."

"I'm glad I don't have that kind of worry. In real life, I mean."

"You can forget about it after she leaves."

"What should I say if she asks about him? If I still worry about it."

"Maybe say he did take off with someone, but like add a twist."

"Like a student?"

"Nah. That's not believable."

"The janitor."

"You probably don't have to worry about a story. She's not going to ask. She's so into herself. Just have to keep her talking. She'll go on about herself easy. She thinks she's so interesting."

"—She's not, though," I cut in. "She's just used to being listened to."

13

Another ten minutes tick by.

Most places don't wait for you when you run late to an appointment. They will have already pulled a walk-in. Or charged full price for a no-show. But I like to give people chances.

The water in the plastic tub is going to cool. I set it at a comfortable temperature. The suds. Most of them have already popped. I stir the water to form new ones. It has to look fluffy when she gets here.

Marla.

I try to think of what else we talked about last time. I don't want to go look in the logbook, to see if there's a note I made to myself.

I hear Marla's voice.

It's loud, and annoying. I'm a little shaken by how loud she is. She has the type of voice, no matter what she says, it always sounds like she's shouting at you.

Marla comes in. Steps on our floor and greets us.

"Everything she says feels like it's in such giant letters," Annie says, closing the bathroom door behind her. I hadn't even noticed when she went in there.

Noi says, "Bet you Miss All-Caps thinks she's quiet."

"No sense of self. Never had to have one," I say.

I tell Marla to pick a colour. I say it again, and she moves toward the wall.

I see the bubbles I have made are good and put my right hand into the water, testing. Not too cold.

I ask Marla how she is.

She says to the wall that things are good. And picks her colours. Orange for her toes and a pale pink for her hands. She walks over, takes off her heels, and lifts herself into the chair. Her toes are brought to me, and I notice something on the side of the big left toe.

A blister.

Last week, a guy came in booked under the name Roger. When he came in, he walked around. His gait was strange. He kicked out his legs side to side—not a quick walker was my guess.

"Who is this fool?" Mai observed.

"All hail," I said. "A king has arrived."

We say that together when a man arrives and we haven't seen him here before.

He wanted a sports pedicure. That is, no polish. Just trimming the nail, filing off the dead skin, cuticle oil, moisturize.

You can't just say it's a pedicure without polish, you've got to add the idea of sports to it. Like sport is a man thing. Even in a place I own, even when I'm in charge, I have to pull my punches. The fact that I am a woman feels like I've already landed a knockout punch.

I thought, at the time, Annie would probably be done in twenty minutes. We like sports manis and pedis. It's easier to get them in and out, in and out. There's no top coat, no colour to pick, no waiting to see if it's dry. And there isn't much talk.

But it didn't work out that way.

Roger is the type of person no matter what you do, he'll take the time to give you a one-star rating on Google. I hate that rating system. You can be doing good for years and then one one-star brings it all down. It's better to be average.

Happy people never fill those things out anyway. It's the unhappy. They are the most vocal. They're desperate to tell. Desperate to hold back even that last full star just because they can. *I'd give it a five, but the place just wasn't my vibe.*

"Ow," I'd heard Roger say. "What the fuck!"

I looked over at Annie to see if she had it under control. She looked nervous and her hands were shaking, and then she said, looking over at me, "He has a blister."

"You work around it," I said, curling my palm and moving my elbow so I made a curve tracing a magnified blister.

She must have just begun scrubbing at his feet. I could understand that. But she's supposed to feel for bumps before she starts anything. Sometimes you can't see blisters, but you can feel them there.

Annie should have asked Roger if he had any problem areas he might want to mention before she began working on him. Speak now, or forever hold your peace. But she didn't.

I went over to help Annie. I explained about the blister and how he should have mentioned it when he first walked in here.

He thought I was saying it was his fault.

I explained again.

He didn't want to hear it, and struggled out of his chair and began to put on his sandals. He hauled himself up and pulled open the door. He made a left and stood in front of our store window and gave us two middle fingers, one from each hand. I imagined, then, his fingers broken. Twisted little twigs. Breaking at all the joints. Even broken, they would mean the same thing—that gesture.

All of us returned the gesture. There were three of us in the shop so that's six middle fingers at him. He was obviously outnumbered. Frustrated, he threw up his arms and walked away.

Soon as he left, I eyed the lock on the door. Wondered

if I should walk over there and lock it. Just for an hour. Enough time, maybe, for him to cool off.

I worry he might come back. To have the last word, to have the final say.

I ask Marla if there's anything I need to know about her feet. As she nods her head, I think of Roger's two middle fingers bumping our window like birds who can't tell there's glass there.

I give a swift glance to the lock, then quickly shift to the front window to see if anyone might be coming for the door. Three leaps and I can be there. Three leaps.

I check the clock.

She tells me her big toe. On the left. The nail is growing and it's catching the skin underneath it.

She doesn't mention the blister. Around it are two other blisters. People don't notice they have them sometimes. Especially if they haven't broken. They look like a small mouth has blown a little balloon here, but if you look closely, there isn't a mouth at all. They look fragile, too, like if you poked at them, they would pop. But they are actually quite mighty. I look closer and see liquid inside the little balloon. It means it just formed a few hours ago. I work around the blisters, and I push the skin below her nails gently back.

Marla turns her phone around and shows me a picture of a baby. It's a video clip of it just a few days old and, already, it seems fed up with the world. Two of its little fists are curled tight under its chin. The baby looks at the people around it, and rolls its eyes and closes them tight as if it doesn't want to see anyone there.

She lowers her voice so only I can hear her. Tells me it's some stranger. People take photos and videos of their babies and post them. They go in real close. You get to experience them getting ready or waking up in the morning. Her favourite ones are when they unbundle them in the morning and the baby does a little stretch.

She smiles lovingly at the phone. She scrolls along and finds another to show me. And I pipe up with something about the kid being adorable.

Marla had a miscarriage. It was her fifth one. A few months ago, she told me that this last one was difficult. She was three months along. The longest she's carried one. The doctors said she shouldn't try anymore.

I have never wanted to be a mother, but that doesn't mean I don't think about it or wonder what kind of mother I would have been. I would've been a great mother. Been mothering myself all my life. Telling myself it's going to be okay, you'll get through this, and that I can do anything, just try. I saw a child's bike on the sidewalk one time. Its three little wheels. Just left there. And I wanted to take it home with me, but what for? No one there to make use of it.

And suddenly I felt a sadness. That we get one life and sometimes in that life we're just not going to get to do everything. And in this life, I understood, that was something I wasn't going to get to do. It's a grief, but for something you never even had or even loved. That was a difference between me and Marla. She wanted them, and she was being told not to want. It doesn't change your want, though. It's still there.

I don't know what it is. Maybe I'm getting soft—and because Marla's been here so often and has told me about herself, I want to make things better for her. Give her hope. Or want her to still want the things she wants. I tell her about something I read in a magazine. A man. He's fifty-one. He'd said, the baby will come when it's ready, and it did.

She asks is his wife fifty-one, or is he?

I think about the story. It actually said he was fifty, and his wife was fifty-one. The reporter also said they were getting a divorce. It wasn't clear if the baby was the wife's. There's a baby now, but not necessarily his wife's, so there's a divorce. All three exist, not necessarily together, but does it matter? What am I doing here? Giving a book report? The story was that he was fifty and there's a baby now.

I repeat that she's fifty-one.

Mai always listens in on my conversations and helps me along when she can kind of guess I'm having some trouble with the chit-chat. She offers, "Tell her about Mr. Pickles. That ninety-year-old thing became a dad for the first time."

I turn to tell Mai and say, "But that's a turtle," and look back at Marla's face to see if she's listening to me. She's scrolling on her phone. I add, "She's no turtle."

"Well, I don't know about that. I mean look at her neck," Mai points with her nose. "It is hot as hell outside, middle of summer, and she's wearing a turtleneck." Mai gives me a little smile, laughing at her cleverness. "And look at the fabric around the neck, all saggy," she says, pointing out the facts to me. "Her neck isn't long enough to stretch it out."

"She might think I'm terrible," I say, thinking ahead, and suddenly worried now about her feelings, "if I compare her situation to a turtle."

"Yeah. But it's just a story." Mai lifts herself up from the desk. Walks over to the nail polish wall and says to the nail polish bottles, "Tell it to her this way, if she says 'They're turtles.' That you feel it's a sign from the universe. She'll think it's some sage advice. People assume whatever we say is wise. We can tell them to eat shit and they'll believe there's a benefit to it." She picks a nail polish bottle from the wall and gathers a few others in her hand. I know she sees they're almost empty too and will go and fill them up.

"I don't know," I say, thinking of how I might be reassuring. "Mr. Pickles is male. I think she wants to hear something she can relate to. A female situation. And it's not like Mr. Pickles busted out those eggs. It was Mrs. Pickles. Is Mrs. Pickles ninety, too?"

"No. She's close, though. Fifty-three."

"Damn." I want to laugh, but I keep a straight face. I don't want Marla to think we are talking about her even though we are. "Even with turtles, they get with the ones half their age!"

I scrape the skin from the bottom of Marla's feet. Careful to avoid going near the blister. Her toes wriggle around. At this angle, they look like the tops of little mushrooms.

Her four fingers form a place under her phone to rest. Her thumb moves bottom to top on the screen about three times, then she puts it face down on her lap.

She looks at the traffic outside. There are other things out there, but I can tell she notices the families. We notice what we don't have. Mothers with small children in their arms, strapped to them, or in carriages. Even a young woman walking alone. The possibility *that woman* has that some day she has before her, she can choose.

I feel myself grow sad, and suddenly want to hide them all from Marla.

She tells me just because she never had them doesn't mean they're not hers. They are all her children. Every time she sees a baby, she thinks they were born to the right parent. They're loved. They will be fine. Even if they didn't come from her.

Sometimes people tell you things and you don't have to say anything. You don't have to try to help them. It's the telling, letting them say it, that matters.

This is such a time.

She asks about Bob.

"Miscarriage," Mai reminds me to say. "Jar in the kitchen." Then she swipes the air in front of her and says, "No, no. He left you. Ran off with the janitor. Ran off with the janitor will get us a big tip. It's more pitiful. You don't want weird. Weird won't get you any tips."

I mutter something about his teaching.

Marla looks at me like she's caught on to me about Bob. I tap her leg so she can give me her other foot to work on. And she does.

Marla notices my finger. Puts both her eyes there and even though she doesn't reach out to touch me there, it is as if she has.

14

The smell of nail polish becomes faint. The smell tells me where I am like a compass pointing north. And when I'm not around it, I want it. When you know something long enough, and you get used to it, it becomes less alive to you. You begin to miss how new everything feels because you can't feel it now. Only way to get rid of that pang is to go outside and come back in.

I stand in front of our window. Feel the sun on my face and tilt my nose toward it. I am not supposed to do this. To let my face get damaged this way. I have freckles, dots across my nose and cheeks like an overripe banana. They're all natural, though they seemed to appear overnight. I have twenty-five freckles. I counted. I like to keep track.

There are three pigeons around me. Pecking. I don't do anything about them. I don't have feed with me. They'll know that soon enough.

I reach into my pocket and I look through Murch's posts. The new girl. She doesn't know it yet. All teeth now, but she'll be spit out too when the time comes. She might go long, and the longer she's at it, the more it will hurt to leave it all behind. You do something long enough and you don't remember what else you can do. They all love you, until they don't.

A pigeon comes near me and I bring my leg up as if to kick, but I pull back. It doesn't know that I mean no harm. Probably just sees me coming close and on instinct decides something about me. The pigeon hops into the busy street. It dodges a few cars, then stands on a streetcar track. I look left and see one sliding fast toward it.

Damn thing. It didn't even move out of the way.

I blink and that grey clump of feathers is still there. That's how I know it's done.

Then a car follows over it. Another car. The pigeon looks flattened now. I can't see the blood from here.

Another car.

I don't know why, but I run out there. If cars honk at me, I don't hear them. I stand there and look at it. Sliced up on one side. A clot of red like it crushed raspberries with its body. The feathers are burgundy-grey. Both feet curled up. Two tips of my fingers grab a foot. I pick it up like that and bring its body back to the curb. But then I don't want to leave it there, near our door within a client's view. I pick it up again and put it in the space between our building and the next.

It doesn't move.

She didn't move either. That girl.

I tested the ropes, the floor. The girl in the ring with me was built like a brick wall. I looked around the ring and there wasn't much of a crowd. I had seen more people waiting for the bus.

Protect yourselves at all times, I heard the referee say.

I blocked a blow. Tired her out. She'd been six steps to my three. I'd read the books Murch gave me. Watched the tapes. I took a shot. She slipped my shots. I took another. She didn't follow up. Jab, jab, jab. You can win a fight with just a jab. Just live in this space. Jab.

Her head. I'd hit there.

She was on the floor. Didn't move. I stood over her. Ready. She might bounce up. Attack. But she didn't move. She didn't look right. Mangled like a body dropped from above.

She didn't move.

I take a deep breath.

I feel like my head has been knocked back, like I'm in the ring and someone has thrown one at me. I tell myself that someone else can come take care of this dead thing. I've got to get back. The girls need me to run the ship.

The air is hot. Exhaust fills my lungs. And I go back inside to the girls. I take another lungful. Excited I can smell the polish, like I have opened a bottle and stuck my nose right over it.

I go wash my hands. Soap.

I look for the things I know will be there to steady myself. I count. Five chairs, four stations, centrepiece. Lotions, towels, wax, disinfectant. Nail polish, filled to the top.

I look at the girls and wonder if they saw me carry that pigeon back. I don't think they did. They don't look outside as much as I do when they are in here. They work, or they talk to each other. I keep them busy.

"Who've we got coming in?" I ask, moving on and reminding us to watch the clock and to pay attention to the schedule.

"No one until two," Mai says, over at the centrepiece, with no computer screen or logbook in front of her, remembering all of this from a single glance and the memory of that.

"We have to get some walk-ins," I order.

"How do we get them?" Noi asks. She is now seated in the chair we have there. Annie's back is to me and she's sitting on the desk.

"We hand out some flyers," I say to Noi. "We go to the coffee shops. Tell them we got a combo special. Two-for-one. Mani-pedi. If they think too long or make excuses, tell them ten dollars. Special deal."

Mai, near me now, complains, "It's hot. And I'm wearing black. I don't want to stand out there."

I bring my eyes back to Noi. "—And you, you far along on the appointments? They confirm? Left messages? That's how we get walk-ins too. They bring friends."

I look back at Mai and address her complaint. "It is hot outside. You're right. Just do it for ten minutes. We'll take turns."

Wax pot, confirming the switch is still on.

I hand Mai a few flyers.

I hear the phone calls.

Two minutes later, a woman with a stroller comes inside. She just wants a pedicure.

The girls tell her to pick a colour. Noi says it first, once. I move to remind Noi to say it twice, but before I do, Annie repeats it. Only then does the woman go to our wall. I look at Noi and show two fingers to remind her we have to say it twice. They don't hear us the first time.

I take the woman to a chair.

Her name's Mary, she tells me. Her under-eyes are puffy and dark. I should suggest a facial, but I'll just keep it to the pedicure. It was years ago, but I hear Rachel instructing me, "You can't just look at someone's face and tell them what they need! You can suggest it if she's pointed it out herself, or if she asked you about it."

Before she sits down, she takes the baby from the stroller and cradles it in her arms. Says his name is Michael. Sits down on the chair and unbuttons her top and feeds him.

I glance at Mai, outside now. She complains, but she always does what needs to be done.

I tell Mary to soak her feet.

Mary puts her feet into the warm water. And sighs. She asks me if I have kids.

She doesn't give me an in to answer.

She says even if I had them, it wouldn't mean I'd love them. They come out, and there they are. Their own person. You think you're going to love them, she says, but she feels nothing.

I like her right away. She makes sense to me.

I look at the baby, how it eats from her chest. Its mouth looks like a hole of never-ending want. Probably cries all the time. And you spend all day trying to figure out why.

Her arms are tired, she says. She doesn't get enough sleep. Doesn't see her friends. And she misses work.

Anyone can be a mother, I think. A lot of people are mothers, and you don't get paid for any of it. Seems like a lifetime internship. You never know if you're doing things right, and someone is always telling you the ways you're doing it wrong.

Here at the shop, I do what I want and make what I want. Everyone I see needs me and when it gets to be too much, I get them out. At the end of the day, they all go back to where they come from. And if they don't, I can shove them out.

Mary says she made six figures. And loved her job.

Seems like the baby is going to eat all that up too. That's the kind of money that makes someone grow up to be lazy if someone else is there to provide. The kind who kills you for your insurance. Or puts you in a home and waits for you to die so they can collect insurance while you lie there shitting your pants in a pool of urine.

I massage her ankles and tell her I don't have kids.

She tells me I'm lucky. And I can see her point, but I don't want to rub it in.

A few minutes pass, and she tells me she thinks her husband is having an affair with the nanny, too. She thinks they fool around when she's asleep, or when they take the baby to the park together.

Mary doesn't know I am talking to her when I say to Noi, "It's probably true," in our language, as if I just told Noi to make phone calls and book appointments.

I dig out the dirt from Mary's toenails and wipe it on a cotton pad like it is peanut butter from a jar.

Noi looks over at me and listens. Then turns her eyes back to the screen in front of her. She doesn't want to join because she has a baby too, and with a man who isn't hers. Not that there's any shame in that, you have what you get yourself into. Who knows what the man might have said or promised. That he'd never felt this way before. That his marriage was over, maybe.

But it never really is, is it.

I scoop a small plastic spoon into the jar of body scrub and spread it on Mary's feet. I bought it for the shop because it promises you can smell paradise all year long. Most exfoliants promise a glow—but paradise, and all year long? That's something I want clients to have.

I don't reassure Mary about her worry even though I know that's what she wants. I am sure she has friends to talk to over brunch, maybe a therapist, but you don't want to tell your friends stuff like this. Want to keep up the appearance of what everyone thinks happiness should look like. After a while your friends are his friends, too. So they're not really your friends. And a therapist would just take notes. Better to tell me. I am no one to her. It's easier that way.

Who am I to say anything about her husband and that nanny? I don't know any of them.

But I do know people.

I think people have good instincts. If they feel something is going on, it probably is. I get that an imagination can run wild, but Mary's feelings about it are so alive to her. Clichéd, even. But a thing becomes a cliché because it's happened so often.

I also think if it's not happening like you imagine, then it's happening in some other universe. I don't think those images we get in our head come from nothing. It's happening, in this moment, or true for some other lifetime or universe somewhere else. We're never wrong.

I ask her what she would do if it were true.

She'd feel relieved, she says. Just being right about it.

I pick up the colour Mary wants, the one she picked from our wall. A sparkly blue.

Mai comes in from the heat. I am not near her, but I can feel the summer on her. Warm, sweaty, close. I ask the girls in the shop, "Is it just me," I bend down to paint Mary's big toe, "but do these toes look like fingers?"

I turn my head toward Noi and Annie, who are at the desk together mumbling about something on the computer screen, and they look at what I have in my hands.

Mai comes to stand behind me and pretends she's giving instructions and leans close to my right ear and says, "Damn. Those things can probably play the piano."

"Ladies and gentlemen. Ladies and gentlemen. Over here, over here. All eyes on me," I say, keeping the sound of my sentences bland and boring so I sound like I too am just giving instructions. "Can I have your attention, please. You know what I've got myself here?"

I pick up the toe next to the big toe.

Noi and Annie smile at me, eyes alert and shining, like I am about to pull a rabbit from a hat.

"Finger-toes!" I say, presenting the reveal, keeping a straight face, but Noi gives me away and giggles.

It's sad that Mary doesn't know our language. Not a lot of people do. I feel sorry for her, if you want to know.

She seems like she could use a friend. And we might even be friends.

Mary asks me what I just said about her. She pulls down her shirt so the baby doesn't take any more. She acts like I have seen too much of her. Her face closes up like a door, but I have already walked through and looked around.

She thinks I am talking about her. She's certain.

I tell her we were just agreeing that the colour she picked looks very beautiful on her. Perfect, really.

And my eyes move on.

15

I am always aware of the clock, whether or not I am looking at it. I can tell by the look of traffic. It had let up a bit, and now it's beginning to fill up out there again. I look over to the wall, at the clock's two hands. One over the other in a single gesture. Reminds me of a middle finger.

I tell the girls to grab lunch before the rush.

"C'mon, you," Mai says, referring to Noi, "big sis will take you out to lunch to celebrate. It's your first day." She sees Annie's face fall. "You too, Annie. We'll both take her."

She's probably going to take them to the little taco place a few doors down. It is nice there. There are two seats out front, a few more inside. But its true beauty is the little courtyard full of flowers. The food there is served in small portions so you always ask for more.

"You want us to grab you anything?" Mai asks me.

"I've got something," I say.

I flip open the logbook, wanting to look busy. I don't want them to know that I want to join them. I don't know why. I don't know why I can't tell them something as easy as I want to join. I've been like this to them for so long, I can't just go and change that now.

They all leave.

I look down at the next appointment. Janet.

The woman is a fan of that place a few blocks from here—Bird and Spa salon. That brother-and-sister team. Janet has a face that's familiar to fashion magazines and the movies. Most people would agree Janet is beautiful but I wouldn't say so. She isn't beautiful, she's familiar. When you see a face you have seen so often, you don't even look at it anymore. Nothing to make your eyes stop and stare at the details and how they have come together. Nothing to slowly take in and store in your mind to call up for later when you want to remember that you saw something that made you pause.

Janet is used to getting attention and holding it. When she speaks, her sentences don't stop. They start unhurried and they meander and spiral around, never getting to a point. She thinks she has something to say because people are looking at her, but after a while their eyes wander to the things behind her or closer to themselves. They aren't paying attention. They are just looking. She doesn't know the difference and thinks it's attention.

Janet fills the air between her and everyone else, and takes up space with ease. She comes in here buzzing around my floor telling me how to improve my place, where to get clients, what I should do better.

Helpful. That's the word she likes to use. Just trying to be helpful. It's more like poking. Poke, poke, poke. Keep poking around, lady. And find out.

She's always telling me what they're doing right with their business over there at the other nail salon. How it's so hard for her to book an appointment there, so she comes here. Her backup. Her second choice. The place that's less busy. She can say whatever she wants. Whatever they are doing over there, she is the one who comes back to us. And we take her in.

There's a figure outside our window.

I look at him. His back is to me. His clothes are ragged and dirty. But he has a regal air about him. He looks like a professor, really. Has a trench coat on. But his skin. The skin on the back of his neck is all burnt by the sun. Nowhere to hide.

I gave him a container of leftovers once. He opened the box, looked inside, and turned his nose up, said, "I don't think so." Another time, I gave him fresh fruit in a paper bag. He looked inside at the two apples and a banana and said, "I will let him know," like he was working at the front desk of his own mind.

He turns around. Looks me right in the eye. I don't know anything about his life, but I can feel the sadness there. I grab a water bottle from our fridge and bring it out to him.

He twists open the cap and starts drinking. I don't know why, but I want to do more.

I ask him if he wants to come inside. I tell him we're doing a special promotion. A free shave, a free mani-pedi.

He trusts me, and comes inside.

I tell him to sit in the white leather chair, the centrepiece. I don't tell him to pick a colour. His nails are long and yellow. I bring the plastic tub to him, and he removes his shoes and socks. Wash, towel, cut, and file.

He lies back like he's done this before and I trim chunks of white hair. And go in to shave closer.

When we are done, he walks to the door and turns back around. He gives me one bow.

One bow.

Then he looks over at my missing finger. Smiles, and says that things must be rough in my line of business. He doesn't ask what happened, why it isn't there. He just takes it as it is, acknowledges its absence, and moves on.

If I told the girls they'd never believe me. If I tell Mai she'll be furious, say I got played. She'd say something like, "I told you to take a walk-in, but a walk-in that pays."

Quick loud *pop-pop-pop*s burst in my ear.

I don't know what it is or where it's coming from, and think, This is it, isn't it? This is how it ends for me. Alone, and in the shop.

I look down at my body. Look for the holes. See if I have been hit with anything. The glass from the window and door are still in one piece. And I tell myself I am safe. I am fine.

It's nothing.

I look outside in the direction of that sound. It's a car. Slowly going down the street. It must have blown a tire. It stops at our corner and the driver looks distressed. A teenager. She comes out and discovers the wheel that's busted, and searches around for help.

Because I'm looking, she heads right for the shop. Asks me if I can help her. She left her phone at home.

I go to the computer and bring up some phone numbers, and suggest a tow truck.

She takes a seat at my station. Biting her nails, eyes buzzing around, lower lip trembling.

I ask her if there's someone she wants me to call, and she tells me her dad. They talk on the phone. He will come by, she tells me.

I think of the water bottles in the fridge. I offer her one and she takes it. Gulps it down quickly. That's one water bottle I hadn't planned on giving away. She's not a client, but she could be.

She doesn't say thanks or anything like that. Someone who is used to other people offering help. A given.

I don't want her here, but I can't tell her to leave. That's the problem with being a shop. Anyone can just walk in and whether or not you are what they are looking for you have to let them look. You can't choose them.

I go over to my station and move my tools around to make it seem like I am not available.

I hear a voice.

It says, "Yoo-hoo!" I know who it is. No one greets me like that but Janet.

I'm told of the weather. Sweat-soaked.

I don't say anything.

Janet looks over at the busted-tire girl and back at me. Annoyed. Janet thinks I have fallen behind in my appointments and I might have to take her an hour from now. She always assumes the worst about me. It's hard to prove to someone you aren't something they think you are. It's a negative they have, and it's hard to come back from a negative.

I point to a seat.

As soon as Janet takes a seat, she has something to say about the business and how I have things. She looks at me from the top of my head to the heels of my feet and asks me if maybe we might think of wearing something other than black. Apparently, the colour doesn't bring the idea of cheer to her.

We wear black because we want to. I like clothes I can just throw on and not think about. If there's a stain somewhere it isn't on my mind.

I click on our go-away-please music soundtrack.

I ask Janet to put her toes in the plastic tub. I ask her if the temperature is all right for her. And I tap her left leg, and she puts it before me to be worked on.

Janet gushes about Raymond. The guy who works at the other nail salon, she says, thinking she's telling me something I don't know. She suggests I drop by there. She tells me they're good people. Good people.

I want her to stop talking about them, or at least comparing us. Don't like hearing about how great they are over there. I'd rather she just go to them or book her appointments there. I feel she's just here to tell me everything I am not by praising them. Parents do that with their children. They talk about one with pride and excitement. It sounds good because it's all so positive and loving, but it's a sly way of putting down the one they don't mention.

I think of something to tell Janet. I want to blow up her praises. Then I smile, because I know I've got it. I tell her there's a fungus outbreak over there at the Bird and Spa salon that they're not telling people about.

She draws in her breath and holds it there, and a hand is brought up to her chest. So dramatic.

I look at her toes. I have to admit, they are beautiful, and she doesn't need much work from me beyond a polish. I tap the nail on her left big toe. Two times. Gently. If I did it once, it wouldn't feel like I had an important point to make. If I did it three times or more, it's too much, and she wouldn't trust me. There is nothing wrong with this big toe, but I lean in close to it, squinting my eyes, and then pull myself back. I make my eyebrow hairs try to reach for each other, but the space between them is impossible so a mound of skin forms. I bring my lips together and try to make the shape of a circle. I then tell her there's a strange colour there that I haven't noticed on her before.

Better get that checked out, I tell her.

When we are done, I follow Janet to the door and wonder if I should lock it. Then I think about the busted-tire girl and her father coming and decide to do nothing.

I look through the glass to a few steps from me.

The pigeon I brought back from the street earlier is out there too. A ball of grey feathers just out front. It is dead. No way about it. Next to it is a living one, and the living one walks around in circles.

There isn't any language, but I can tell by the circles it is making that the thing might have meant something to it. That it recognizes they're the same in some way. Mai circles me like that on the floor every day.

It's how I know I am alive.

16

When the Susans return, the girl with the flat tire is still sitting here.

Mai comes in and looks the girl flush in the face, but the girl doesn't feel her stare. She's not someone who's used to feeling like she doesn't belong someplace, and if she ever does feel that way she is someone who expects others to make her feel welcome.

I explain to Mai what happened earlier.

"So? Why is she sitting here?" she asks me impatiently. Before I can answer her, she spits out at the girl, "We're not car mechanics." Mai's head weaves in small tight circles. The girl looks at her blankly, because she doesn't know our language, and looks away.

"Dad's coming to pick her up," I say.

Mai's eyes are still on the girl, looking her up and down, but the girl can't feel her heat. Mai pulls back and dismisses her with a flick of her hand. "Must be nice," she says, and moves to the back room, her voice trailing bitterly, "to have Daddy come rescue you."

Noi and Annie follow in and pass Mai coming from the back room. Mai doesn't shrink herself in the short hallway. She takes up the space she wants and the two girls rub shoulders with the wall. Mai comes out to the floor and notices the water bottle in the girl's hand and says, "And you gave *her* one too?" She is not happy about all this. She walks over to the centrepiece, turns her back to me, and stares outside. "So how long do you think it'll take before her dad gets here? She's probably going to use our toilet. How about some food for her? Oh, a bed for tonight. Roll out the red carpet for her, why don't you." She spins her face to me, arms folded tight across her chest.

She doesn't like people who come into the salon and take up space without paying up for anything. Sometimes she forgets she's not in charge. I kind of like that. It feels personal to her, and I can let myself relax. I don't always have to take the lead or say the thing that I'm thinking. She knows. They say people can't read your mind. Mai gets pretty close to it, for me.

I vaguely remember who is coming in at two, and open the logbook. Mai blurts out, like she's seeing the logbook through my eyes, "It's someone new." I love how she looks ahead, and knows what's coming up, and has a great memory like this. Makes me trust her. I don't trust a lot of people. It's how I've always been. It's easier that way.

Noi and Annie come from the back room too and huddle around the desk. Annie shows Noi how to replace the roll of paper in the receipt machine.

I look at the name in the logbook, and she's right.

New clients take a lot. It's harder to get them in and out. Tell them to pick a colour and they stand there longer than you want. Plus, I have got to get to know them. What they want. Why they are here, what they are hoping for. And, I have to get them to want to come back—and with a group of friends, of course. Whenever anyone new comes in here we like to ask about their lives. What they do, who they're with, who they want to be with, do they have a family, are they happy.

It's good for business to know these things.

If they have money, we suggest more services. They don't like to look cheap to us. If they don't have anyone, we press on that. Get them to think if they wear that serum, that nail polish colour, have their eyebrows shaped that way, then their life will change in an instant. They will be aligned with the universe.

Easiest money to make are people who are single. They aren't spending it on anyone, and so they have a little more to spend on themselves. And they'll do anything—anything, I tell you—if you can help them imagine not being alone anymore.

Vanessa. Eyebrows.

Doesn't say threaded or waxed. Thread is better. More precise, no chemicals. Wax might irritate the skin. It's no different to the client sometimes, but I have to know which because a wax requires the wax pot to be ready.

And does she want to be called Vanessa? Or is that the name she gave because it matches the credit card which holds her appointment? Maybe she wants to be called Ness or Nessa or Sa. We'll see.

First eyebrows are difficult.

Do they want a natural full look, do they want a prominent arc, do they want them tinted? I will have to ask her to fill out the form so I know what she puts on her face. Make sure what I put on her face isn't a bad mix.

I remember the wax pot. It should be on ... and it is.

This one time a Susan wanted to see me sweat and turned the wax pot off for giggles when we had the client down for it. So I gave my speech about the virtues of threading but they walked out. I don't like walk-outs. There's no receipt for a walk-out. No proof that I was there. No record of the work I did.

Thing is, though, like I told Noi, they always come back. Even the ones who complain about us. They come back. All we have to say is: Ten dollars. We can do a mani-pedi for ten dollars. We can wax for ten dollars. It's how we get them in and out, in and out, and coming back.

The front door opens.

I don't know who it is. This must be Vanessa, I think. I will have to do a lot of talking so she knows what's happening. Since she's new to our shop.

The woman tells us her name.

It is Vanessa, and I tell her she's with me. I remember to smile. I don't usually, but she's a new client, and how they see you first always sticks with them.

She makes her way to the centrepiece and I ask her if she's wearing any makeup or has had a facial peel in the last three days.

She has makeup on her face and no peels.

I test Noi and call over to her, asking, "When do you put toner on someone's face?"

"After you cleanse," she says quickly.

"She has makeup on. So you double cleanse before the toner?"

"Yeah. Double cleanse, then the toner."

I can tell Mai wants me to be warmer toward Noi. It's her first day and I'm not easy on first days. I feel if they come back after the first day, they will come back the days after. I shouldn't have to be warm and nice to get the girls to come in to work. It's not a playground where you run around and ask anyone to be friends. This is a business. In and out, in and out. And that goes for the girls too, if they don't have what it takes.

Annie comes closer to Noi and whispers, "It takes a while for her to warm up to someone." She strokes her hair, and says, "She's not as bad as she comes across."

I don't want to join in on what they have going on over there, and change the subject:

"She doesn't have full brows." I pretend to wipe my own brow as if I am fixing the hairs into place. "She fills them in herself."

Back still to the window, arms still crossed, Mai observes and adds, "I can tell from here. The severe lines." She sticks out a hip toward busted-tire girl as if that small movement could push her out the door into the street. "You should tell her to do it properly."

"First time, though."

"Suggest a tint. Saves time. Don't have to fill it in yourself. Might as well. She's here."

I pump makeup remover onto the cotton pad. It is odourless and colourless. It looks like water and feels like water and smells like water, but it is not. I begin wiping her brows but her head leans back like a bobble head. She doesn't know she's supposed to lean toward me. This is why you talk to them. To get them to work with you.

Vanessa adjusts and leans into the pressure.

She tells me she prefers to be called Van.

I think, Oh, didn't see that coming. Most like to shorten their name by using a chunk of the middle letters or a chunk at the end. I didn't think anyone wanted to be called anything like a vehicle.

"Like the car?" Mai says, throwing her voice into my ear again. "Why would you take a good name like that and want to be called a van?"

Annie chimes in from her place at the desk, "Ask her who she's driving today!"

"Did she get her brakes checked?" Noi adds.

I say, "How many does she seat?"

"Does she have four-wheel drive?"

"Is it difficult getting a parking space?"

"She's pulling in right now!"

"How many miles has she got on her?"

We have taken our joke as far as it can go, and stop. Van can't tell we are joking about her name. It sounds like we are just having a conversation among ourselves. We are, she's just at the centre of it.

I tell Van I am going to mix the colours.

I apply the colour to Van's brows to tint them. I wait twenty seconds and check the colour to see if it's dark enough and it seems to have taken.

I remove the colour.

Take out the little hairs on her eyelid with wax strips, and clean up the shape of the brow with tweezers. As I begin with the tweezers, I notice the skin around the eyebrow is turning pink. That's normal. The skin after a wax is sensitive.

Van tells me she has trouble sleeping.

Her neighbours are having such loud sex. They do it around ten-thirty or so every night. It's like clockwork.

"Probably trying for a baby," Annie, still at the desk, says.

Van thinks they're trying for a baby. And hopes so. So they stop doing it so much.

"Don't know about that. Sometimes having a baby or being pregnant makes you want to do it more," Noi says, typing something up on the computer. Annie looks at the screen with her, and writes something down in the logbook.

I wonder if Noi felt that way. Having been pregnant, and had a baby.

"The time they'll need for it to line back up again," I say to the girls. "Months."

Mai, cleaning my tools now and handing me one, says, "That's if it came out of there. And if she's a healer. There can be complications. You never can tell."

"You're never the same after," Noi tells us. "Your body, or the way you see it."

Van says she knows their sounds shouldn't keep her up. It's just she feels like they're right there in the room. Too close.

I don't say anything.

She says she's single, so it's not like she can make the same noises for them to hear.

They don't know that, I say.

She laughs.

She looks at her hands. All five fingers in each hand pressed together, all alert and lined up as if for duty. The skin is dry and dull. Her nails are bare.

I ask her if she wants us to do her nails.

Another time, she tells me.

I am a little disappointed by that. She won't get to see my missing finger because when you work on their face, they close their eyes.

I like it when someone notices.

Van tells me her ex-boyfriend used to tell her she was asking for too much. She just wanted to see him more than once a week... and this woman next door, she's getting to do this every night. It's not like *she's* being told she wants too much.

"I don't know about that," Mai says, doubtful. "Maybe the woman was told she's too much, but she does it anyway. You can do that, you know. When he says, 'I've got to get up early in the morning,' just do him." She walks over to a chair at a station and spreads apart both her legs and lowers herself onto the seat. "He won't be getting up early for anything when I'm finished."

Van hasn't seen any of this. Her eyes are still closed. The girls at the desk hold back their laughter, and Annie says to Mai, "Might as well just do it when you have them there. They're going to disappear anyway. Who cares if it's asking too much."

"Just get yours," Mai says.

Vanessa doesn't think the guy next door loves his girlfriend. It's only been two weeks. Maybe she'll be gone soon.

"Who says it's his girlfriend?" Mai asks. "Could be just a friend."

"Isn't that what they always tell you?" Annie says. "That they're just friends? And hanging out. One of the guys. Would you believe it, though? This one-of-the-guys shit. 'Why isn't she hanging out with me instead?' is the thing I'm thinking."

"It's because you ain't got a dick," Mai points out coldly. "And that's what she wants."

I ask Vanessa how she knows that he doesn't love her.

She says it's because it's all they do over there.

"A fucking performance," Mai says bitterly. "Who screams like that for that long? It's a show, for him. All that grunting. Like come already. I have stuff to do."

Suddenly, the girls all look at the door. A man is there, and pulls it open. I am already there, tools still in my hands, and he steps back and says, "Whoa, whoa." Holds both palms up and slowly backs away from the door. His eyes dart away quickly behind me—and points to busted-tire girl who walks quickly to him, passing me.

I almost forgot the girl because she isn't going to produce a receipt.

When I turn back in, all the girls look at me.

Mai is the first to speak. She says, "You still thinking about Roger?"

I don't say anything, but she knows.

"You scared he'll come back and do something to us?" She doesn't leave room for me to answer. Her eyes go to the busted-tire girl outside, and she says, "That girl. Bringing things in here to scare the shit out of you. After everything we did for her."

Haven't been this ready to go since my boxing days. Murch had to drill into me not to be scared. He'd squeeze my arm and say, "You are stronger than you look. Don't got to be afraid of nothing here."

I look at the lock, the door, the sidewalk, across the street into the park.

17

I am outside again.

Standing by the sandwich board. Leave the girls in there to sweep and clean up. Leave them to talk, if they want, without my eyes on them.

I lift my eyes to the hydro lines across the street. There's a bird sitting on one of them. It's not a pigeon. It's smaller. The lines look like some kid took a black crayon and tried making a straight line. Two, three times. Even when I am not thinking of them, Nok's kids come into my mind like this. I worry about them, where they are, what it will be like for them. Then I remember I have my own life. And whatever happens to them, they are with their mother.

I take a deep breath and clear my lungs. I miss the smell of polish, and I go back inside.

Soon as I walk in, one of them teases, saying, "Pick a colour! Pick a colour!"

Everyone knows we can't pick a colour for ourselves.

But there they are on the wall. Waiting. Still, I walk over to the wall. See which colour draws me close.

I like this lavender colour. If I could pick a colour, I would pick that one. I look down at my hands. How dry and wrinkled they look. I don't have nice nails. But I don't do anything to change that. I'm always on the other side, doing the work to make others look good.

But that's where I want to be.

"Say it twice!" Annie says sternly. Her eyebrows make an effort to come together but do not meet in the middle. "They don't hear you the first time."

Before I know it, Annie's come over and linked an arm around mine and Noi follows her and does this too on the other side and we look like a charm bracelet. They carry me over to the centrepiece and Mai is there, ready to go. She pulls the thread taut in her hand, acting like a professional killer in a movie about to strangle a neck.

"Boy fen," Mai says to me, roughly. "You hap one?"

I laugh.

But she remains serious and says, "What so fun knee?"

And then she breaks, and laughs too.

"He hap money?" Annie says, also in a fake accent. She comes close to my face and says, "You know, ah, ah," her right hand spinning something invisible like a Rolodex, pretending to search for a word, a way to explain what it means to have money, "a goot job?"

Getting back into character, and as if I have been arrested and taken to a holding room, Mai says forcefully, and towering over me, "He may-lee you?"

I am a little stunned by her seriousness and my laughter dies down a little.

"Why, he no lope you?" Annie says with concern, as if I was really a customer. "He not marry you. He no lope you," she quickly sums up.

Mai runs a finger gently along my upper lip, the cupid's bow, tracing something as if it were there. She says, "No, no. Too much. Man no like," she waves a pointed finger at me, adding, "No good. This why you hap no boy fen."

We don't really talk like this. We're talking like how our clients imagine we talk.

"No bay bee!" Annie continues, incredulous. She tosses both hands up like it's obvious. "How he may-lee you now. Aiiieee," she spins around like she doesn't have time for someone who doesn't know the basics, and looks out the window like a general commanding troops with a strategic plan. "You gip him kid he may-lee you. Stay wit you foe-evah." When she gets to her last word it sounds like she is a magician and has just cut through a wooden box and split it apart without any blood, the body intact and still moving. Pointing to the magic. FOE-EVAH.

Noi has been brushing my hair delicately this whole time. The teeth of the comb just on the top stray strands.

"So pretty, pretty," she says. But there's something about the way she says it that doesn't seem like she's pretending or playing.

I have been called so many things. Tough, strong, brave, a force. But not pretty. I realize no one's ever said that to me before, and meant it for real.

I am in the centrepiece and I look at all four of us in a side mirror above the sink. How alike we are, what we do. I don't know if the girls love it. Maybe Mai does. I don't want to do anything else. The thought of being somewhere else, doing something else, without this place, these girls to pass the time with, and I feel like I don't even exist.

"Hey, before I forget," Mai says, stopping everything, and pointing to the back room with her whole hand. "Just wanted you to know we bought you lunch. Left it in the fridge."

"Oh, thanks."

"I know you like to be all in charge, and take care of everything, but you should come eat with us. Maybe just once. It'll be fun."

"Yeah. Sure," I say.

I want to join sometimes, but I don't want to get to know them. Makes the job harder. They'll start to come in later, take less care with clients, ask for things. When you're in charge, you have to keep your distance to keep the place running.

I get up from the centrepiece and we each fall back into our spots in the shop.

I join Noi and Annie at the desk, glance at the computer screen and don't see any appointments. There might be a walk-in, but it looks like I should grab a bite now.

On the back table, there's a bowl of rice with broccoli and a fried egg sunny side up. The yellow a perfect circle. I didn't tell them to bring me anything. There's a pop can, too, still nice and cool. There's a straw tucked underneath the metal tab.

I don't want them to know I wanted this. I don't tell them thanks. I don't tell them I want anything. I was hungry. And they thought of me.

Murch would call that weak. "Don't ever let anyone see you want. Don't you go looking for their pity. Pity don't pay."

I think the girls probably talk about me behind my back. I don't know for sure. I would, if I were them. I can imagine Mai would be the first to say something, give the girls permission to speak freely. Over a plate of tacos, she might say, "See how she just grabbed my hair and cut it? Like what is that."

"Why do we have to look like each other? That's so fucking creepy."

"And no, we don't have to say 'Pick a colour' twice. They can hear it the first time."

"Does anyone here know what happened to her finger?"

"Probably cut it off herself."

"Got up one day and said, 'Fuck this,' and just did it. So people stop asking questions."

"I mean what if someone wants to marry her? Like how do they put a ring on it?"

"It's like she's married to the place. Has nothing else going on."

"Wouldn't even know what to do with it if it was there right in front of her."

"Get your paycheque, girls, and just go home."

"That's all I'm doing."

"That's probably what Nok did. Except she was smart, asking for a bunch and taking off with it."

"Made a fool out of her."

"And we got to take care of it. Work our asses off."

I shake my head and remind myself that their talking behind my back is fine with me. As long as it stays behind my back. I don't need to know. It's how they bond with each other. Talking about me. Having some common thing to say to each other.

I look up and notice the bathroom light is on. It should be turned off when no one is in there.

Flick.

Off.

I feel the air move. Someone's come in, I think. I rush out to the floor and see who it is.

But it's no one.

Mai asks me, "Hey, you eat?"

I don't answer that and go up to her, say quietly, "I might cut Annie. Thinking about it."

She doesn't try to talk me out of it. She asks, "You think we could get a guy this time?"

"Think we could be killing it with the tips, huh."

"We need a Raymond."

"A guy's not hungry. Worst kind of worker, someone who's not hungry."

Murch said girls in boxing were hungry, and that made them more pure. He would say something like, if I'm remembering right:

"I hate to admit that, but it's true. You bring in big ideas of purses, television, sponsorship deals, the movies, and you tarnish the sport. It can get you all of those things, but you forget about the sport. The respect you show your opponent, how to get your opponent to respect you with nothing but your footwork or with one punch, bam, to the face. It's that direct and blunt. Respect. If sometimes I'm hard, it's because I know more than anyone else that it's going to be hard for you out there.

"If I don't get you to be right, you'll go turn on me, and say I ain't doing my job. Even if I'm doing my job, it could get to feeling I'm too rough, too cruel. But it ain't me who is cruel. It's the system. I'm just telling you how it is, how it's going to be. I work you hard and dash dreams too because I don't want my fighters dreaming of the big time. They've got to love the sport, the hours outside of the ring, that they put in getting there. They've got to love that. Else there just ain't anything to love."

"I want something," Mai says, "besides you girls to look at."

After ten minutes passes, she looks over and says to me, "Going out for a smoke. Come with?"

When we are outside, our backs lean against the window. I look over at Mai, and watch her like I think she's beautiful. She taps the cigarette and bits of ash drop like a flock of birds. Her eyes are brown like mine and when we're in the sun like this they look like honey. I don't have to look anywhere else to know what my eyes look like. I can see hers as mine.

It doesn't take long before one pigeon comes at me. And then a few others. The pigeons think I've got feed, a crumb of something to throw down at them. I don't want them anywhere near the entrance. Get enough around and there's a crowd. And then you've got their shit all over the place.

"Annie's shift is over," I say.

"She showed up today when we needed her. And in ten minutes," Mai says. "Last week wasn't her fault. The client had a blister."

"What's so hard about spotting the blister before working on him, though?"

Now I've got to watch that door all day and worry if I should be locking it. Turning to it each time there's some noise. Even when there's nothing but a change in shadow.

I don't usually let a girl go.

It's a really difficult job. The things you have to know, and how we work. Once you're in you're in, and usually we do what we can to keep you in. Nothing, though, can prepare you for the real thing. The real face. The real toes and hands. Every one of them is different. Our job is to make them look the same.

Some need more work than others and then it's just about maintaining after that. This job isn't just the job. It's looking after each other, too. Sometimes watching someone not use common sense puts the rest of us at risk.

"I might cut back her hours later in the week."

"She's not ready to work on the weekends or during rush hour. Her time is best used in the morning. There's less people and it's a lot easier to work then."

"That's what I'll do. I won't get rid of her."

"Give her a chance. Let her work her way back."

"And anyway, I have to remember about Nok."

"Yeah. It's because Annie works those shifts that Nok even has a chance to come back to something. Not surprised. With a name like that. Seems destined." Nok means bird in our language. Mai says, "She got close to you, huh. Probably them kids, too."

"It's not like her."

"Happens. People. They disappear on you. Don't give it more thought. We'll hire a new one."

I don't say anything and she can hear what I mean without saying it.

"You knew her for like what, a couple of months? That don't make knowing her."

I kick at the pigeons.

I'm careful not to touch any of them. Just enough for them to feel the air I'm kicking, and before I touch, I pull back. It's just like working on a punching bag. You don't go with full force to make the land, you just touch. You ruin your shoulder that way, going full force. You have to save all that for the ring.

I can tell the pigeons apart. There are three here. That one has a pattern of marble stone across its middle. And that one has a deep purple near its neck. Almost like a jewel. And that one there has a soft grey that turns dark near its tail.

I have a feeling, and look up.

18

The first thing I notice is a circle of black fabric slipping by me. She doesn't notice me there, but I've stepped out of the way so she doesn't have to. I take whoever comes. I follow her in, and Mai joins me.

I hear the walk-in greet everyone. The front desk, the empty chair, and me.

"She's so loud," Mai says.

"I know," I say, dryly. I look at the walk-in's small mouth. Surprised sounds so loud can come out of there. "Thing is, she has no idea."

"Must be related to Miss All-Caps," I say, decisively. "Sis All-Caps."

"Ah-ha. Good one," Mai approves, repeating, "Sis All-Caps."

Noi has caught on to our name for the walk-in, and takes it up like it has always been the woman's name. She says, "Sis All-Caps wants to get her nails done."

I remind Noi what she's supposed to say. Pick a colour.

Twice.

Suddenly, I notice something in Sis All-Caps's hand. She shows us the bottle, holding it at the top, and wiggles it around like stirring something in a big pot.

I look at the colour she has chosen. A dull grey.

I keep my voice steady and arrange the tone to sound industrious and boring like I am just asking for one of my tools, and say, "She wants her nails to look dead?"

Annie appears, all packed up and on her way out, and when she gets to the door turns to all of us and says, "Not my problem anymore. Shift's over. I'm out," and brings a flattened hand up to her temple for a salute.

Noi thanks Annie for her help, and comes back to me, says, "Should we suggest another colour to her?"

Mai looks at me, and switches the bottle of moisturizer at my station to a fuller one. "Why?" she says, with a smirk. "Looks like she knows what she wants."

I look at the new bottle and I am happy. I imagine this is what a car might feel like when it's run empty on gas and it's been filled.

The woman plops herself into a chair, and gets right to it like she's known us for years. The bubbles haven't even formed in the water yet and she's already started.

She tells us about a man. He's married, though. She thinks he wants out of it.

I listen for a bit, and say to the girls, "I don't know

why people get hopeful about Marrieds. I mean, they're married. Why get involved?"

"It's the rescue thing," Mai volunteers. "We think we can rescue them."

She pauses for a while, and then says, bored, "They can rescue themselves." Marrieds like to come after her. They come in here with their wives and slip her their phone numbers when they pay. Or they come back a few days later looking to buy a gift certificate and slip her their numbers then.

"Why do you think people get married these days?" I ask. And the girls all give a bunch of reasons at the same time:

"Too scared to go after the one they really wanted. So this one will do."

"Because Mother approved of it and life's easier when Mother agrees."

"Hung around long enough. He had to do something."

None of us in the shop are married.

"Must be nice," I say. "Dating when married. You get to go home to someone when you get rejected or dumped. Who would ever leave that?"

I glance quickly at Noi, and see that she's not looking at me. She was with a Married. Don't want to put her on the spot.

I point to the little bubbles foaming below the woman and she puts her bare toes in. I ask if the temperature is all right for her.

I think she's been here before.

Something about the way she knew to go to the wall even before we told her to pick a colour. The way she went straight to the chair. I think she's always a walk-in. Never makes an appointment. Comes when she wants. On her own schedule. Wants to be squeezed in.

I think about her question about Marrieds. How I should answer.

I want to tell this woman not to get involved, but she is here with her toes and hoping.

I ask her if she gets a Married, how will she trust him?

She doesn't reply. Thinking.

From what I have seen with my clients who do get involved in situations like this, it turns out that married people tend to always go back. Other times, you are only there to help them see they don't want to be married. And when they get out, they go for someone else.

Of course, it also depends on how long the guy's been married and if he has kids. If it's ten or more years and there are kids, then you're taking everyone in. Nothing's really completely yours.

Marrieds want you to tell them what to do. That will be the relationship. You're always telling them what to do, trying to convince them. Then when they leave, if they leave, they leave you too, for someone who doesn't tell them what to do.

I think people who get their nails done are hopeful. They think they can do something about things. They think things can change. That they can try harder.

I try to find out more.

She tells me an affair can sometimes bring people closer together. An affair helps a marriage.

"Tell yourself that, lady," Mai says to the walk-in. She walks over to the nail polish wall and straightens some of the bottles. "I mean if they can have you on the side, for a good time, and not blow anything up, why not keep things as they are?"

I file down a small bump on her smallest left toe. It's the middle toe for her. Her smallest toe. It somehow has grown different, never quite caught up in length to the others. The one left behind.

I put a serum where I've filed.

The walk-in says you're just there to get two stupid people to realize they love each other, maybe. She says this man puts in time and money to make himself look good. But his wife is just this lump. And he's still there.

"Damn," Mai says quietly. "If *that* ain't love, I don't know what is."

I ask the woman if that might be true love? Knowing you could be somewhere else, wanting to be somewhere else with someone else and... and deciding to stay?

She shrugs.

I lean down to pick up the colour she chose from the wall.

One of the girls says, "Leaving is true love. You free yourself. You, plus the one you're with, the friends you always complain to about the same things. And you're free to feel whatever you want." I know it's Noi who says that. The sound of her voice. Scared and a bit shy, but certain from experience.

I shake the bottle in my hand and begin to paint.

Misery is probably more intimate, I think. You're miserable, but at least you know it. And the other person does, too. Both of you still staying together such that no one else can have that misery. Only the two of you know it together.

The walk-in interrupts my thinking.

She says she's doing all this skin care stuff which costs her a fortune. All this makeup. Spends so much on clothes and all along she could just be wearing sweatpants. And do nothing about those sagging bags under her eyes.

I look at the area under her eyes. They don't look like bags and they don't look like there's any sag there. I can't see her pores. Her brows are clean and shaped.

She says his wife is a lump, and she wishes she could just be a lump too, and that someone could love her for that. She uses that word again, *lump*. I think for a moment about that, and don't really understand what she means. Aren't we all just a bunch of lumps anyway? I nod along.

She comes around again. Says it never works out. All roads lead back to he and his wife being together.

"A one-night stand," Mai says, imagining. "And he feels so guilty he goes back. Embarrassed. Then grateful she would take him back."

"They always take them back," Noi chips in. "You might have a year with him at most. Or a few months. When he's had his fun. And if it goes on for a while, how can you trust him? If he does it to her, he can do it to you."

The walk-in says the Married has children, too. She looks at her own hands and turns them around as if she can read her own palms.

"They've made memories that she'll never have," Mai says to me.

She tells us the man's fifty-two.

"Forget it. He's past his prime. He's got nothing to offer at that age," I say to Mai like she is the one who asked me for advice. I say, after a moment, "Wisdom, maybe. But I've got that, too."

Mai looks out the window, brings her eyes to the door and the lock. She says to it, "He's not exactly a young thing. Probably will slump over in a few years if he doesn't lose all his hair in three. Meanwhile," she takes a moment to calculate, "the wife had the best years with him. It's over even before it's begun."

I ask if his wife is rich.

She tells me that his wife comes from generations of money. They have a house in the city, another place they rent out. And she's tenured at the university.

"Ah, he'll never leave, then. No one leaves a rich bitch. She can get anyone to stay with her money," Mai says to me. She explains, "Rich is better than beautiful. It's as good as forever. You can always get beautiful on the side."

The walk-in asks me what Mai is saying. I tell her we think she should do what she wants. It's not a lie.

I look at her face. Square with a short forehead, small pointy nose. Lips like someone painted a single line in her face. There's a sadness she carries there. Not very confident. Always asking others for reassurance. It's why the Married can work her.

This walk-in's name has a word like *lean* in it, I think. Eye-lean. It makes me think of my optometrist. He puts a few drops of liquid into my eyes and they don't blink when he brings the machine up close. Every time I visit him, he tells me to lean my face forward and rest my chin on the pad.

I try not to look at his face, try not to look into his eyes, but they are there looking at mine. I always try to make conversation and get to know him. I ask about his weekend, but he keeps the talk focused on what's at hand. He tells me to read letters on the projector.

The letters start off looking like dots and I guess from their shape what they look like. When I get them wrong, he doesn't tell me. He moves in, something clicks, and everything in front of me gets clear. I want to know about him, want him to tell me something to agree with, to see his point of view and his feelings, but he's not in my chair.

I'm in his.

When he tells me the exam is done, I don't know where to put my eyes so I look at his arms. The tightness of his shirt. He's someone who spends time at the gym, working on that look. It doesn't happen just sitting around on the couch. Probably likes the usual—tall, leggy blondes. Probably thinks I look like one of his sisters, our shiny black hair.

It's a relief, really, not to be anything to anyone. If he leaves me, he's supposed to. He isn't mine. There weren't promises made. If he doesn't come home, I don't have to think of where he's been and with whom. If he mentions someone pretty, I don't have to ask if I am too. I can look how I want, and can love that myself.

Eye-lean. Aileen. Eileen. That's her name.

She asks us if she should date or just be happy.

We say all together that she should just be happy.

She tells us he'd probably want a sex fest if he got out of it, and not a relationship, being married that long.

I tell her she can be part of that fest, but she says she doesn't want to share. She is a one-at-a-time kind of girl.

"Tell this walk-in to shove a few in there, and the right one will come along," Mai says, and we break out laughing together.

The woman looks at us, not knowing what we said. I take pity on her and tell her.

Eileen. I think that's her name. Eileen leans back and laughs. Her laughter starts out alone, then foams and bubbles around the room to us, and we help her and add ours to it.

I look at her smallest toe in my hand and it wriggles around as if it's laughing too. I wonder if she knows it does that sometimes. I look up at her face, and wonder what happened to her that she can't tell she is happy already.

19

Mai is the first to leave me.

I can feel it happen before it does. I don't look at the clock, and we don't say anything to each other. Everything sounds slow and faint inside the shop. There are no nail polish bottles at our stations or with the chairs against the wall. The tools look shinier.

Mai wipes down the centrepiece, sweeps around it, and heads to the back for her things. When she comes back out, she notices me watching her from the window and smiles at me sadly. She pulls at the door and leaves.

She didn't change into clothes for outside the shop. She is still wearing her work clothes. I look at her hair, and remember suddenly that I had cut it this morning, and she let me. I want to run after her, get her to come back, but it's important to let the girls go. To get some distance from this place. They aren't like me. And I don't want them to be. It's better that way, if you ask me.

I know she lives with her mother, and I begin to

wonder about that woman. If they look like each other. Do they get along? Or is her mother as real as my Bob? Just something to give to someone so they think things about you.

I wonder if Mai talks about her job here or mentions me to her mother when she gets home. What will she tell her mother about the bridal party today—what did she notice about Lizzie's toes, hands, and face that I hadn't been close enough to see? Will she mention how the pitcher asked about getting a "happy ending" again, or mention Roger? Will she mention what happened with Noi at lunch, what they talked about, what they ate?

I want to know, then realize there are some things I don't need to know. I was there. I saw it all. There are receipts printed and filed in a drawer that back me up. Mai's eyes are just as good as mine. We look at and work on the same things. When I give in and become a sound in the shop she becomes one too.

I look over at Noi then, and wonder if she needs to be told she can go home now.

First-days need to be told that. She looks busy typing something up on the computer and then writing it into the logbook. Moving to sort out the receipts.

I say to Noi, "You can go home now."

She looks back at me and at the clock. She nods, and puts the receipts back in the drawer. She goes to the back room for her things and just before she pulls on the door to go out, she turns around and says, "Your finger," pointing her nose to it. "You don't have to tell me what happened."

I have been watching her work all day, and haven't noticed her take a look at it. I don't say anything because I know. I don't have to tell her what happened. It doesn't matter. It happened. And that's all there is to it.

Noi then says, "It's more interesting that way. Not to know."

It really doesn't interest me to tell. I just like waiting for someone to notice it. Says a lot about people and who they are, more than it does about me.

I wonder now if she will come back. You never can tell with first-days. I try not to get too close or have expectations about them. She did seem to get along with the girls, and joined in real easy when she wanted to.

She's told me she has a baby. But she didn't mention anything about it today. Mothers always want to tell you about their baby. If it sleeps, when it needs a diaper change. That young, I wonder who's been taking care of it while she was here working all day. She didn't show me a picture. Maybe the baby was her Bob. Something to make up to get the job and begin right away. Most jobs take a few weeks before you can get started. I can start someone right on the spot. Who wouldn't want that if they needed the work?

You never can tell with people. About who they say they are and who they really are. And over time, they change—not because they lied about themselves. They just changed, that's all. And they aren't that anymore.

I watch her walk the opposite way from where Mai went. Her little steps outside the shop are the same as when she's in the shop. She doesn't change how she walks out there. Mai walks different when she leaves the shop. All her ease goes away and she speeds everything up. When she enters a crowd of people, she takes their speed as her own. Doesn't hurry up to break through or hang back to avoid being pulled in.

I reach out to touch the window.

A faint warmth. Means the day will end, and I have to bring everything to a close.

Most people like this time of day, and look forward to it. I don't. Reminds me of watching fireworks—that moment when you've been enjoying all those pops and bangs, and then there's a pause in the dark, and you know the show is probably almost over.

I don't like to live in that pause.

I fill this time out with work. And if I don't have it, I start making calls. I arrange the nail polish bottles along the wall. I take out the tools from the blue liquid and wipe them down. I take out the garbage, clean the bathroom. Put out a new roll of toilet paper. I like for the toilet paper to look like it's a brand-new roll, and not down to its last few squares.

Someone walks by, and I see their feet. Open toes. Long yellow nails. A cracked heel. I can't reach down and help, but I want to. I want to so bad. I feel myself want it so bad, it feels like a kind of panic.

I forget that I can't do anything for some people. That they go on like that. With their nails. Chipped. Unaligned. Uncut. Cut too short. Not buffed or polished. And no one asking you to do anything for them. They don't even see that something needs to be done! I want to point, to shake everyone to tell them to make an appointment! Please.

I should go out there with some flyers. I would say Here, here, and Here, here, you too, you take this now. Here. Come see me. We'll work out a schedule, a plan. We can work together to get you back on track. Here. It doesn't have to be this way. Don't you know?

Pick a colour! Pick a colour!

People walk around the outside world like this and without shame. I want to rip the wall of nail polish out and drag it with me everywhere I go. Set. Ready to work. To help all these fools walking around. Pick a colour, pick a colour. Please. Pick a colour.

I try not to look at a face.

Pores probably the size of quarters. And hair everywhere. Growing out of every hole. Pluck. Tweeze. Wax. I want to do it all. Get every one of them out. At the root. And the eyebrows. That carpet on everyone's face. That bush of hair. Have they no decency! There must be space between the brows. Come see me. Please. I can help. Heck, I will do it for free. It doesn't have to be this way. I'm telling you it doesn't have to be this way.

I look out the window again.

A group. The cracked heels. Oils, please. Let me rub this in. It will be all right. Temperature. Is the temperature okay? Not too warm, is it? I want to seat everyone on our centrepiece. Spin them round and round until it all blurs.

One person at a time. We get one person at a time. Can't do them all at once.

I see movement by the door, and my neck turns swiftly.

I have an uneasy feeling about Roger coming back. That feeling doesn't leave.

Any loud noise, any drop, every time the door opens, even when the phone rings. I look out the window again and walk to the door. I have my eye on the lock. I turn the lock. To make sure. Make sure the lock does click into place. Doesn't get jammed. In an emergency, things like that happen. Locks don't turn. Locks don't click into place when you need them to. Just checking. I think of turning the lock back, but I am alone.

I keep it closed.

The lock jiggles.

Someone on the other side.

I adjust my vision. Her face was known to me for so many years. There's no mistaking it for someone else's. She's here. Rachel.

20

I let her in.

Rachel pulls at the door and when she's opened it wide enough for herself she comes in. I take a few steps back to give her room to take what I have made all in. I wait for her to say something. Anything, really. But she does not. My shop is smaller than hers, and we offer the basics. When people want fake nails or paintings or anything complicated that might take up three hours we tell them to go to hers. When we don't like them, we tell them to go to her shop then, too.

I remind myself I am alone on the floor. The girls have all gone home. The place is empty. I try to see this place like it's new to me, through Rachel's eyes, and it doesn't look like anything worth bragging about. I can't tell her to come back another time. I have nothing to point to and say, "I'm busy," or that business is booming. I have no girls around me to point to.

I don't know why she is at my shop. She's never come by before. Maybe she has caught on to us, about me telling people who love her place so much that there's a fungus outbreak over there.

She looks me up and down, and I let her.

She surprises me, and says flatly and slowly, "Ten dollars." It's our secret—me and the girls here. We offer it to clients who won't come back to us. Anyone fussy, ready to complain about our services or prices. We never lose one, like I said.

I nod, and say, "Pick a colour."

I think about saying it twice like I always tell the girls to, but I can tell I don't need to. She heard me the first time.

She brings one to me.

The colour is beautiful. It is a shade somewhere between lavender, pink, and pearl. It isn't a bold colour, but it's a colour that gets the eye like bold colours do.

Rachel chose a chair along the wall, and not the centrepiece where I would have pictured her sitting. Doesn't matter where she sits, she looks regal anywhere. I fill the plastic tub with warm water and soap and bring it over to my chair. I place the tub below Rachel, who is already sitting there, and point into it.

We don't say anything to each other the whole time. It's because we know each other. And maybe when you know each other like this, there's not much to say.

Rachel rolls up the hem of her pants, right up to her knee, brings a leg up and pulls off a shoe, and she does the same with the other side. I am nervous suddenly because it is the first time I will see her feet. It's so intimate to see someone's feet. Even when you're naked with someone, you don't get to see their feet. This is more bare than that.

I look at her toes.

None of the smaller ones are longer or bigger than the big one. And I look at her hands too. She has a nice nail bed. They look great to begin with. It won't matter if you shape them square or oval. Not a lot of people have that. She's someone who knows what she has got, and she doesn't need to be told.

I quickly bring my eyes to her face and look for the beauty mark I remember on her lip. And it is still there. When she yelled instructions at me when she trained me, I would stare at it. When she doesn't say anything now I look at it too.

I come back to what I have in my hand. I have her feet and feel for blisters and bumps. For things I have to work on or work around, or let her know about. She does not have these things I have to tell her about.

I don't have to cut or file. I just have to wash, scrub, and paint. I scoop water from below her and bring it to both her shins. I don't need to ask her if the water temperature is all right for her. This is the temperature she gives all her clients.

I work in the body scrub between her toes. The skin there looks a bit dull. She is a busy person and she wouldn't spend much time doing that for herself in private. Probably hops in and out of a shower. Not a person who has time for a soak in a bath.

I notice hair on her toes.

I quickly look up at her, but her eyes are closed. I move to shave the hair. She isn't looking at what I am doing at all. And I do it with a lightness that she can't feel.

I begin to relax a little.

When you work on someone who knows the ins and outs of your job, it can make you nervous. You overthink. You have your own thoughts and instincts and they crowd up next to what you think they are thinking. It's so easy to begin with the wrong step, to do things out of order, to drop a tool, to forget. I am surprised she trusts me enough to not look at what I am doing. That she has her eyes closed.

Hadn't noticed it before, but her feet are really tiny. When I hold both of them in my hands, her heels rest at the tips of my fingers and her toes don't go all that far past my wrists. I place them gently in front of me and wipe off the wet.

I moisturize, spending time around her ankles. When I worked for her, she always complained about how they hurt her. Even though she says nothing to me now, I can imagine her voice saying, "I wish a motherfucker would," if

I made a move to ask her if she wanted a foot massage. I am already pulling out stress from the joints.

Since we aren't talking, my ear wanders and finds sounds. Her gentle breathing, the hum of the air conditioner, the computer's grunt. Further on out, I hear the wheels of cars on the pavement. Their speed. A streetcar. I see a flash of red on our walls from an ambulance that doesn't have its siren on. I can hear my own heart beat loud in my chest. It feels like there is a Ping-Pong ball in there.

There is a birthmark the size and shape of a nipple near her ankle. And, I see a small scar just below her knee. Did she fall off a bike when she was younger? Maybe when she was learning to ride it without its training wheels. Or was it something someone did to her? A fight with her brother, maybe. I want her to tell me about the scar, but she isn't open like that the way clients can be.

There isn't a lot of space between her toes. I roll up toilet paper and thread it between them. We don't use that sponge they make. It's cheating, if you ask me. When we can just do this. Less waste, and less cost.

I feel my body on alert, ready to jump away if she were to make a sudden move. If she got up and started pushing my chest. She always did that to me when I worked for her. Because you worked for her, were in her territory, she felt she had permission to push you around.

I thought she would say:

"You talking about me, huh? Think I'm stupid, don't you? Think I am not going to know what you tell everyone about me?"

I heard then what I have always been told.

Protect yourself at all times. It's been years, but I can feel my body remember. And even though Murch isn't here in the shop, I can hear his voice in my ear:

"Don't just tag her. Whip. Whip your jabs. Push from your leg up. Your leg is behind the power in the punch. No one remembers a tag. Pulverize her."

It didn't matter who was in the ring. I just looked at the centre where the collarbones came to meet. That little curve there. Kept my eye there. Can't let her see you plan or think. Don't think. Move. Shuffle, breathe slow, elbows up.

I eye that spot on Rachel's neck.

My body is always ready for a fight, even when there isn't one. I don't talk about it, but I remember every fight I had in the ring. All of them. Detail by detail.

I landed everything easy. I waited to see the dot of red underneath their nostrils. An eye puff up. Murch was always there. A look away. Steps away. A voice called at me, "You gonna be gentle up there? We expect that from girls. Ahhhahha." It was Tony, the other coach.

Murch didn't laugh.

"Get the fuck out, Tony. Don't be talking to my girl and messing her up. She's better than those dildos you've got. You'll see."

Murch rushed to the door and shoved Tony's face out and the rest of Tony's body fumbled and followed. One shove. Two.

I could see Murch's back. Tony stepped away from Murch's shadow so I could see him clear. He lifted his flat breasts. Pointed to me. And said, "I'm here to see you in a bag. It's gonna happen some day. And I'm here to see it. Ahhha."

Murch took him by the collar and pinned him to a wall like a little insect. His arms and legs struggled and fluttered about. He couldn't get away. His centre, stilled.

Murch was yelling.

"Keep your eyes here." He used two fingers to point with a slight bend, almost a claw. What he was pointing to was a spot below the neck, the centre, right under the chin there.

"You see everything when you look here. You see his feet. How he's moving. Where he's going to come from. Look here, always."

It was a good thing I am alone and Annie isn't here. The girl's still scared of her. Rachel might have gone up and cornered her here in the shop and said something like, "Couldn't get out, huh? Coulda done this same shit at my place. But no. I fired your ass, didn't I?"

I move up to Rachel's hands.

They are flexible and can bend quite far back. Especially her thumbs. Almost at a ninety-degree angle.

She is left-handed, too. There is a scar on the finger she uses to point with, the right. To cut yourself there you'd have to be holding the thing with your left. It should have received one or two stitches, but she's stubborn. The type of person who grins and bears it.

We are alike that way. More alike than either of us want to be.

Even though Rachel hasn't said more than a few words to me since she came in here, I know the sound of her voice. Brisk and brutal and quick. If she were a boxer, she's someone who would take you out in the first round. "Why bother going through the other rounds?" would be something she would say.

The skin on her inner wrist is really soft and pretty. I don't know why I would describe it like it's a face and say it's pretty, but when you look at her wrist it gives you the same feeling you would have if you were looking at a face. Something in your eye decides something about it. When you touch her wrist, you want to be gentle to it. And you don't know why.

I have never seen her nails done up like this. I want to ask her why she's here, what all this is being done for. Her life is the shop and her brother. This is the first time I've ever got a look at her outside the shop. She looks different to me, but I don't know what it is.

We wait for her nails to dry.

There is no pressure to talk or to say anything or to start something up or to pretend to be interested. I don't have to draw her out. It is nice to be with someone who is so self-contained they don't need or want anything from you.

Her eyes open. And she blinks a few times. She moves her eyes past me and stares across the street, at the park. People can have their eyes open and be looking at something, but that doesn't mean they are looking at it. Her mind is wandering somewhere the way my ear does in the shop and for the world outside. I wonder who she is thinking of, what voices she hears. And are they kind to her?

I don't tell her that we're done. She knows this.

And she walks over with me, to the desk, and she slips me a ten-dollar bill. She knows cash won't leave a paper trail. That I don't have to enter it anywhere or keep a record. There won't be a receipt for this.

She could say it never happened, that she's never been here at all.

I reach for the cash and I'm embarrassed at the way I do that. I seem desperate and hungry. Sweaty and wet.

And then, something strange happens. As I pull back my arm, she reaches out and slides her hand gently along and then touches my finger. The missing one. Her thumb presses over the space that is there. She moves to hold what is left of my finger, a little round bump, with a gentleness I didn't think she was ever capable of and gives me a kind smile.

Then, she walks out on me.

I don't know why, but I lock the door then and I decide not to let anyone in. I go and stand by the window and look out at everything. I feel myself smile and a warmth unfolds inside me. It is like a tight coil has come undone somewhere and I know it's safe to turn it loose. I reach for my finger, for where I have been touched by her. There is so much light now. Maybe too much. And I wait. Wait for the dark to come in to me.

ACKNOWLEDGEMENTS

Thank you to Sarah Chalfant at The Wylie Agency. Jessica Bullock. Bonnie McKiernan. Jean Garnett. Liese Mayer at Little, Brown. Sally Kim. Angelique Tran Van Sang. Emma Herdman at Bloomsbury UK. Thank you to Kiara Kent at Knopf Canada for making this what it wanted to be. Martha Kanya-Forstner. Kristin Cochrane. Thank you to Keith Hayes for designing this book's cover, getting right her hunger and joy. Laura Jane Wey. Bani de la Rea. Vinh Nguyen. Gökbörü Sarp Tanyildiz. Doretta Lau. Alexander MacLeod. Sarah Bowlin. Cressida Leyshon. To my boxing trainers Mickael Alban and Allan Hernandez at the United Boxing Club in Toronto. Amber Mehboob. Sekai Nail. Toronto Arts Council. Ontario Arts Council Recommenders' and Works in Progress grants. The Canada Council for the Arts. University of Toronto, Massey College Writer in Residence program. University of Winnipeg Carol Shields Writer in Residence program. Saint Mary's University Writer in Residence program in Halifax, Nova Scotia. Southeast Asian Solidarity Collective at the Diasporic Vietnamese American Network.

A NOTE ON THE AUTHOR

Souvankham Thammavongsa is the author of four poetry books and the short story collection, *How to Pronounce Knife*, winner of the 2020 Giller Prize and 2021 Trillium Book Award. Her stories have won an O. Henry Prize and appeared in *The New Yorker*, *Harper's Magazine*, *The Atlantic*, *The Paris Review*, and *Granta*. This is her first novel.